The Art of Healing

a novel

Joan,
I hope you enjoy
reading as much as I
enjoyed writing.
Jeanne Felfe

JEANNE FELFE

PARALLEL PATHWAYS, LLC

The Art of Healing – A Novel
Jeanne Felfe
Copyright © 2016 by Jeanne Felfe

The Art of Healing is a work of fiction. No characters in this novel
are based on real people, living or dead, and any resemblance is
purely coincidental. *The Art of Healing* is set in the real city of
St. Louis, Missouri and the surrounding area. Although some
real-life iconic places are depicted in settings, all situations and
people related to those places are fictional.

Published by Parallel Pathways, LLC
St. Charles, MO (United States of America)

Cover design: Raven Tree Design—www.raventreedesign.com
Cover photo: Garry McMichael—www.garrymcmichael.com
Editor: Heather Rexon-Capewell—
http://raezryans.com/editing-services
Book design: Raven Tree Design—www.raventreedesign.com
Author photo—David Rush

Publisher's Cataloging-in-Publication data

Names: Felfe, Jeanne Marie, author.
Title: The Art of healing : a novel / Jeanne Marie Felfe.
Description: St. Charles, MO: Parallel Pathways, LLC, 2016.

Identifiers: ISBN 978-0-9670185-1-5 (pbk.) | 978-0-9670185-2-2 (ebook)

Subjects: LCSH Man-woman relationships--Fiction. | Grief-
-Fiction. | Nurses--Fiction. | Photographers--Fiction. | Saint
Louis (Mo.)—Fiction. | Romance fiction. | BISAC FICTION /
Romance / Contemporary | FICTION / Contemporary Women
Classification: LCC PS3606.E3875 A78 2016 | 813.6--dc23

acknowledgements

*W*riting a novel seems like such a solitary thing to do. Sit alone and write. Easy enough, right? Nothing could be further from the truth… it takes a team of individuals to take words and turn them into something worthy of the time it takes to read them.

Where it all started…

The Art of Healing began its life in 2012 as a short story. In July 2013, my friend and fellow writer, Debbie Manber Kupfer, introduced me to NaNoWriMo, a crazy undertaking with the goal of writing 50,000 words in 30 days. Having recently retired, I figured what the heck, and set out to accomplish this monumental task. There were only two problems… up to this point, I'd never written more than a 2,000 word short story, and I had no ideas for a novel. The last day of June, while working in my garden, Julianne, the female character from the short story, began a conversation in my head with what became my main male character, Jokob. He insisted his name was indeed Jokob (pronounced Jah cub), not Jacob, and that his nickname was Joko. They proceeded to share their love story with me. I flew through about 21,000 words in the two weeks I had, monumental given my previous writing history. So my first thank you is to Debbie for roping me into NaNo. I don't know if I would have ever completed a novel without your push into the deep end.

As I struggled to turn 21,000 words into a full-length novel, my earliest readers and my critique partners kept me going and helped tame the beast. Thank you so much to all of you.

Sharon Hepburn—thank you for reading that first mangled mess and finding plot holes large enough to drive a Jeep through, and for helping me understand the world of nursing and Italians.

Diane How, Tammy Coan Lough and Matthew Swoboda—you were my first critique group. You helped me hone my craft and kept me accountable. Thank you all for reading and re-reading until the story worked.

Saturday Writer's—thank you for providing a safe place to write and learn and for turning me into a published writer.

Saturday Writer's Novel Critique Group—I've learned so much working with you. We're all developing together.

The Fiction Workshop on Facebook: Damien Lutz, Joseph Y. Roberts, Michali Lerner, Paul Draper, RL Andrew, Heather Rexon-Capewell, Shelia Hudnall, and M Nicole Morrow. Your eyes on early chapters helped me polish them to a bright shine. You are my go-to online support, but you all feel like close friends.

Tricia Whelan—you were the first non-writer reader to read the entire manuscript. You helped me add the finishing touches and gave me the confidence to take the next step.

How do I begin to thank my editor, Heather Rexon-Capewell, for her exquisite editing? I'm not sure it's possible. Her style allowed my voice to blossom while still fixing everything that was broken—http://raezryans.com/editing-services

Raven Tree Design provided the beautiful internal formatting as well as the current updated cover design—www.raventreedesign.com

The original gorgeous cover was designed by Cleve Sylcox.

Garry McMichael graciously granted permission to use his sunrise photograph of the Clark Bridge in Alton, IL—http://www.garrymcmichael.com/

Thank you to my son, Justin Boyd, for remembering to ask me every so often how the book was going. And thank you to my steps, Jill and Derek, for being in my life—you remind me that anything is possible.

And thank you to my fur babies—Maisie and Zeeba—for sharing my lap while I typed around you and for understanding in your little doggie brains that sometimes treats have to wait until mommy can finish her thought.

Finally, thank you to my sweetheart, Greg Stricker, for understanding and supporting all the hours I spent with notepad in hand, or in front of my laptop. And for learning when to close the door so his classic rock didn't invade my brain. You are my world. All my love always, in all ways.

I appreciate reviews if you'd like to leave one. If you happen to find an error, please contact me at jeannefelfe@gmail.com or on FB at https://www.facebook.com/author.JeanneFelfe/

To Mom, for instilling in me the passion to write.
I wish you were here to see it.

To Daddy—I miss you more than I have words to express.

Part One

Julianne

one

*J*ulianne rolled over in bed and reached for the warmth of her husband. Her hand met an empty space, already cold. "Clay?" Wondering why he was up so early, she slid to the edge and dangled her feet, patting the floor in search of her house shoes. *Where are they?* She hopped to the floor and lifted the duvet. Not finding them, she pulled on her robe and hobbled on the heels and balls of her bare feet, keeping her toes cramped upward to avoid the frigid hardwood floors. She found them, right where she'd left them inside the bedroom closet.

She hurried down the narrow hallway toward the bathroom and twisted the knob. Locked. *That's weird.* She made haste to the kitchen and popped a coffee-pod into place before heading back to the bedroom. Julianne flipped through her assortment of scrubs, selected a set with yellow and green elephants, and slipped them on. After tossing her nursing shoes into her backpack, she grabbed her sneakers for the walk to work.

Shoes in hand, she walked to the bathroom door and knocked. "Clay, sweetie. I really need in there."

Silence. She tried the knob again. Still locked. She knocked louder. Groaning, she leaned her back against the city-apartment-white wall across from the bathroom and put on her shoes. "Clay?" she called through the door. "Come on, sweetie. Coffee's ready. And if I don't get in there now, I'm gonna pee my pants."

Silence. She pounded on the door. "What's taking you so lo—"

The door swung open and banged against the wall. "There. I'm out." Her husband held up his hands in surrender. "Geez, get a grip."

Julianne blocked his way to the living room, arms crossed over her chest. Tilting her head to the side, she tapped her foot and pursed her mouth. "We've talked about this. Now that I'm back on dayshifts, you have to share the bathroom in the morning."

A frown pulled his eyebrows together in the center, and he slowly shook his head, not a single auburn hair out of place. "Sure, whatever. I gotta go."

Julianne closed her eyes and arched her neck back, lips parted in anticipation of his goodbye kiss.

Clay's lips airbrushed her cheek before he twisted around her, snatched his bag off the couch, and bolted for the door. "I'm outta here." The click of his wingtips echoed off the walls.

Julianne's eyes popped open. Raising her eyebrows, her mouth slackened. "Uh, seriously?" Hands on her hips, she stared at the back of his tailored suit disappearing out the door. *Why am I bothering with a nice dinner? He's become a real jerk since he changed jobs. I liked him much better when he was still a pharmacy tech. This pharmaceutical rep stuff has gone to his pretty boy head.*

Shaking her head, she stepped into the bathroom and stumbled over the pile of wet towels on the pink-tiled floor. Looking at the disarray on the counter, she groaned. *He can clean up his own mess when he gets home. I don't have time for this today.*

She wet her short blonde curls and fluffed them with the blow dryer diffuser, and speed-brushed her teeth. Pausing to stare at her reflection in the mirror, she noted the dark circles under her denim-blue eyes. *I'm so glad my night shifts are finally over. Maybe now I can get more sleep.*

In response to their loud mewing, Julianne padded to the kitchen, her new shoes squeaking on the wood, to feed Ben and Jerry, giving each a quick scratch behind the ears. She grabbed a Power Bar from the pantry and a bottle of tea from the fridge and added them to her backpack. After racing out the door, she took the inside stairs at a gallop. She sped off on a brisk walk to the hospital, passing the ubiquitous three and four-story brownstones that surrounded the hospital in the Central West End. She loved the smattering of single-family homes mixed in among the multi-family dwellings that gave the neighborhood an eclectic vibe. She hoped to save enough to buy one someday.

St. Louis was finally coming out of one of the worst winters on record. For months, her four-block walk to the hospital had been treacherous due to ice, but she dreaded paying the outrageous fare for such a short cab ride. Still, on the worst days, it beat digging her car out from under two feet of snow.

This morning she took full advantage of the pre-spring warm-up and enjoyed her walk. The cardinals, robins, and blue jays tweeted raucously to greet the morning sun. Squirrels darted across her path, oblivious to her impending footfalls, chasing each other in pairs and scampering up the decades-old maples that towered over the street.

Crocuses and daffodils lining the block made Julianne's heart lighter, as she breathed in the crisp air that smelled like sunshine. Bright yellow, they danced like tiny ballerinas in the morning breeze. Finally seeing some color peeking out from the drab, still dormant grass lifted her spirits.

Julianne charted patient notes at the bustling nurses' station. She glanced at the clock on the computer for the umpteenth time. Four-thirty… finally. Her charge-nurse, Barb, had granted her request to leave at five instead of seven, and Julianne was anxious to get going. She thought through her plan again. *Clay gets home around five-thirty, so I should be able to stop and get everything and have dinner ready by six-thirty. That oughta work.*

"Earth to Julianne." Debbie stood in front of her. She was coming on early to relieve her.

"Sorry, did you say something?"

"I asked if you were glad to be back on days," Debbie said.

"Oh. Gawd, yes." Julianne yawned and rubbed her eyes. "Sorry, I haven't been sleeping well during the day. I love nursing and was happy to help out for a few months, but I don't think I'll be doing that again. It was brutal. I don't know how you work nightshifts all the time."

"I actually prefer nights, but I always was a bit of an owl." Debbie leaned against the counter. "So, any special reason to take off early today?"

Julianne's eyes lit up. "Today's the anniversary of mine and Clay's first date, and I have a special dinner planned. Marco put together a meal I can simply pop in the oven when I get home."

"Yummy. Marco's is the best."

"I'm doing all of Clay's favorites—pork loin, au gratin potatoes, green beans almandine, and a German chocolate cake. Plus, I picked up a bottle of Little Hills Traminette—that's what we had that night at their restaurant. I can't believe it's been five years since that date." Julianne sighed and logged off. "Done."

"Does he know?"

"No, it's a surprise." Julianne gathered her things. "We've never celebrated that anniversary, and I decided it was about time. I even bought a sexy little teddy."

"You devil, you." Debbie giggled.

"I'm buttering him up. I've decided that tonight's the night to have the 'I want a baby' talk. When we were dating, he said he wanted kids, but he's never even mentioned it since we got married. Not once in three years." Julianne flipped one hand in the air. "What does he think? They simply show up on your doorstep in a car seat?"

Debbie laughed and headed off in response to a patient call light. "Have fun. Please do all the things I never get to do," she called over her shoulder.

Julianne strolled the three blocks to the market. It wasn't on her way home, more like in the other direction, but Marco cooked the best food in the West End.

The bell on the door chimed with her arrival. Marco's handlebar mustache tilted into a grin. "Jules," he called out. "I've got everything ready for you. I even threw in a little something extra."

Marco's Market was a staple of the neighborhood. Doctors and nurses who worked in the four-hospital complex and med students living in the area comprised most of its clientele. His services far exceeded simple groceries on the shelf. He could also cook almost anything and package it for reheating, or for the freezer.

The market took up the entire bottom floor of a large building. Twelve families lived above the store, including Marco and his wife. They'd considered moving to one of the homes in the nearby upscale area of University City, but chose instead to remain there among their patrons.

"Marco, you're an angel. I don't know what I'd do without you." Julianne stepped around the counter and hugged the man who had become like a second father to her. She stopped in two or three times a week to select fresh food, and he was a regular at her parents' home.

Marco loaded everything into two paper sacks. "Are you sure you can handle all this?"

"I'm good." She patted the top of her thigh. "That's what hips are for," she said. Laughing, she handed him her card. After he rang up her purchases, she picked up the bags, placing one on each hip.

Marco waddled over to open the door. "I sure hope Clay appreciates you." He kissed her on both cheeks.

"Me, too. Love you. Ciao."

By the time Julianne arrived at her apartment, the sun hung low in the sky. Even with the longer days of daylight-saving time, it was still difficult to avoid coming home at dusk. She hefted the bags up the front stairs and breathed a sigh of relief when her neighbor opened the security door as she reached the top.

"Thanks," Julianne said, propping the door with her thigh.

"No prob, just heading out," he said, jogging down the steps and onto the walk.

Julianne struggled up the stairs with her purse and two overflowing paper bags of groceries. *Damn, when will I learn to keep handled bags with me?*

"Clay, honey, open the door!" she yelled, kicking the door. "Clay?" She kicked it again. Silence.

"Harrumph." As she bent to set one bag on the floor, the edge tore, and she barely escaped dumping the whole thing. She rummaged through her purse for her key, unlocked the door, and peered inside the dark room, lit only by streaks of evening light sneaking in through the closed blinds. Her eyes strained to adjust.

Slamming the door with a hip bump, she juggled the bags and moved blindly toward the kitchen island, again cursing the builder for not installing a light switch by the door, instead of on the other side of the kitchen.

"Clayton, I need help in here!" She reached to set the bags on the butcher-block cart. Both bags hit the floor with a crunch and crash, sending cans, bottles, and loose apples rolling in all directions.

Startled, she raced across the room and hit the absurdly installed light switch. She froze, taking a second to register the now empty spot where the cart had been for the past three years.

Julianne gasped, not sure whether to run out of the apartment in terror or into the bedroom to find Clay. Recalling a news story from last night about a rash of break-ins in the neighborhood, fear crept up her spine. She tiptoed from room to room, feeling a little ridiculous, clutching a can of creamed corn over her head. Noting the oddest items missing—in the kitchen, the butcher-block cart and the microwave cart, but not the microwave, which now tilted haphazardly on the counter top; in the living room, the thread-bare blue lounger she hated, and the god-awful talking bass—a sick sense grew in her gut. Confused panic morphed into dread. She raced to the bathroom, almost tripping over the morning towels, and flung open the medicine chest. Gone. All gone. Razor, shaving cream, toothbrush, dental floss, weird hair gel. Gone.

Stunned, Julianne left the medicine chest hanging open and willed herself to the bedroom. Flipping on the light, her gaze fell to a single dingy-white sock on the hardwood floor in front of the partially opened, now empty, dresser drawers. Looking at the rumpled creamy tan duvet, half-on, half-off the bed, her mouth pursed to one side. She distinctly remembered making the bed that morning. On his side of the bed, there was a space where his pillow should have been—on her side, a small scrap of paper in the middle of her pillow. Trembling, she reached for what turned out to be a greasy In-Out Taco receipt. Dazed, she flipped it over.

"Jules, I moved out, but I guess you can see that. I couldn't do it anymore. Thought it'd be easier if I left while you were at work. Clay."

10

Slumping onto the bed, she missed the edge and her butt hit the floor, scraping her back on the lip of the metal frame. With her feet sticking out in front of her, she remained motionless while Ben purred and rubbed his white fluff against her head. Jerry poked his black nose out from under the bed and nuzzled her hand.

Turning the note over, she read off the items of food— two burritos, six tacos, two large sodas—enough food for two. *Didn't even bother to use clean paper*. She crawled to her nightstand, reached for the house phone, and dialed.

"Let…" She cleared her throat, trying to find her voice. "Let me speak to Clay." The words stuck in her throat, like burnt toast.

"Jules," Gary said, followed by a long pause. "Um, he's not here."

"Well, where the hell is he?"

"Um, I don't know."

"Gary, you're his best friend. There's no way in hell you don't know." Her voice barely escaped through clenched teeth as she struggled not to scream.

"He asked me not to say."

"You knew? You knew and said nothing? Did you know last Sunday at dinner? Shit, did Tammy know, too? What the …?" The volume and pitch of her voice increased as she fired question after question. The sickness in her gut rose and singed her throat.

"No. Tammy didn't … doesn't know. Jules, I—"

"I bet you even helped the coward sneak out. I thought you were my friend, too. You bastard!" Screaming, she slammed down the receiver, picked it up, and slammed it again and again. She grabbed the handset and threw it across the room, ripping the cord from the wall, sending Ben streaking in search of a safe haven. She circled in the middle of the room screaming until hoarse, not caring what the neighbors might think.

Unsure of what else to do, she stumbled to the kitchen, picked up the bottle of Traminette from where it had rolled, grabbed a glass, and poured.

The bathroom was dark, except for the glow from a dragonfly night-light, by the time Julianne dragged herself out of a now icy bath, leaving the mostly empty bottle of wine sitting on the edge of the tub. Not bothering to dry off, she rose and the room spun. Tiny goose bumps covered her skin. The beast rose up from her belly and out, and she barely made it to the toilet before hurling until acid bile burned her throat. When she regained the use of her legs, she flipped on the light. She flinched from the brightness and put up a hand to cover her eyes.

Leaning her elbows on the vanity counter, she rinsed her mouth and splashed cold water on her face. Lifting her head, she blinked in the mirror at her swollen eyes. Her curls stuck out in all directions, looking like she'd dried them while standing in a Texas windstorm. A guttural moan that began at her core mutated into a sound she didn't recognize as her own voice. She swiped her hand out and hit the wine glass. It flew off the counter and shattered into pieces on the floor around her feet.

Sobs gurgling in her throat, she stepped away and leaned her bare back against the cold, sweaty wall. Her thighs quivered and gave way as she slid her butt to the floor. She passed out, naked, slumped half on the pile of wet towels, half on the Pepto-Bismol-pink tile.

two

The faint trill of her cell phone tugged Julianne into a semi-conscious state. On the second ring, she jerked her head up abruptly. Her stomach flip-flopped while hammers pounded in her head. The walls and floor seemed to undulate around her. Placing her hands on the icy cold tile to steady herself, she struggled to her knees.

The phone rang again, this time the distinctive ringtone registering in her brain. *Bella.* She patted the pile of wet towels in search of the sound and retrieved her phone from where it lay hidden, muffled under her makeshift bed. She clicked answer and put it on speakerphone.

"Jules! What the heck's going on?" Bella demanded, not waiting for a hello.

Julianne used the sink to pull herself to wobbly legs, aware of a horrid throbbing in her head, made even worse by the intense sun blazing through the open blinds. She sucked on the insides of her mouth, trying to induce some moisture, or at least something that didn't taste like the bottom of her shoe. After grabbing her robe from the hook on the back of the door, she slipped it on and took a step.

Her right foot connected with a large shard of glass. "Shit!" She hobbled to the vanity, ignoring Bella's frantic questions.

"Gonna need stitches. Great, that's just what I need today," Julianne muttered, while Bella rattled on. She dug medical supplies out of the vanity drawer. Careful to avoid stepping on more glass, Julianne placed her wounded foot in the sink and used tweezers to extract the glass. She ran cold water over the cut to flush it, flinching from the sting. Trickles of red swirled around the white sink, painting a weird abstract.

While she dried her foot and pressed pieces of gauze on the wound, Bella continued, "I just ran into Clay. He tried to hide behind the melons, and I swear he acted like he didn't see me. What's going on?"

"He's gone." A tired, heavy sigh escaped Julianne's lips. Her lifelong friend would hound her until she got the rest of the story, so although too numb to volunteer more information, she did anyway.

"Clay left me. Coward moved yesterday while I was at work." She released another heavy sigh.

"What? Oh God, Jules. I had no idea you guys were having problems."

"Ha! Neither did I." Julianne wrapped white medical tape around her foot to hold the gauze in place. She reached for her wet towel and pushed the glass pieces into a single pile on the floor. "Hang on, I've got to get dressed."

She slipped the phone into her robe pocket and hobbled on her heel to the bedroom. Digging through her drawers, she slipped on panties, sweat pants, and a t-shirt, not even bothering with a bra—she rarely wore one of those torturous contraptions anyway. She tried hopping on one foot, but switched back to the heel-hobble, when she discovered hopping caused her head to pound, like a backbeat in a frenzied nightclub. Propelling herself in this manner, she made straight for the living room and collapsed onto the overstuffed recliner couch, allowing the brown microfiber to envelope her.

Julianne pushed out an exasperated sigh. "Okay. I'm back."

"Do you think he's seeing someone else?" Bella asked.

Julianne lay silent on the couch, pondering the question.

"Jules?" Bella persisted.

"That never occurred to me. He's not the type. But if you'd asked me yesterday, I would've said he wasn't the type to up and move out, either."

"Is there anything I can do? I'm coming over."

"No. Don't," Julianne snapped, pausing to rearrange herself on the couch. "I don't want company. Besides, I really do need stitches."

"Stitches? What? Why do you need stitches?"

Julianne groaned at Bella's concerned oblivion. "Didn't you hear anything I said? I cut my foot on a broken wine glass."

"How the heck did you do that?"

"Bella, sometimes you slay me, but it's not important. I have to call nursing services and take off. No way I'm spending a day on my feet with stitches. Ha! And with this hangover, I couldn't deal with all the crying kids. Hanging up now. Later."

Bella tried to interrupt, but Julianne clicked end call before she could say anything else.

Julianne stared at her phone. *What the heck am I supposed to do now?*

Dragging herself off the couch in response to the insistent ache in her foot, and an immediate need to pee, she heel-hobbled back to the bathroom. She stepped around the pile of glass, leaving bright red splats from the blood-soaked bandage on the disgusting pink tile. *Kind of an improvement.* She changed the dressing and put on her purple fuzzy slippers, straining to squeeze the right one on over the gauze. Realizing the two-block walk to the clinic would be impossible, she called a cab, grabbed her purse, and limped down the stairs to wait.

Shavenda looked up from behind the open receptionist area. Julianne grimaced. Although sweet, keeping secrets wasn't one of her higher qualities.

"My Lord, girl. What you done to yourself?"

Julianne looked around the stark, empty waiting room. *I lucked out today.* The free clinic was an extension of the hospital complex designed to reduce strain on the ER. It received United Way funding, often serving the uninsured. The room looked it: plain tan tile floor with some pieces broken, a dozen metal-framed chairs with what barely passed for cushions, and last year's *Urban, Ebony, and Cosmopolitan* magazines. Cardboard boxes lined the walls.

"I broke a glass, and stupid me, stepped on a piece. I need stitches," Julianne said.

"Well, you in luck, we ain't busy. Finally got past all them ice falls." Shavenda twisted her chair sideways to squeeze out of the cramped receptionist area. "Come on back."

18

Shavenda waddled into the exam room, huffing for air, with Julianne limping behind her. Julianne plopped onto a chair and wondered who was on call today. All final-year residents were required to take shifts at the clinic as part of their training. Many of the nurses also worked there for extra money.

"So a piece of glass got the better of you?" The doctor offered his hand, but he stopped with his head tilted to one side. He wagged a finger at her. "I wasn't expecting to see *you* here." A grin crept across his face.

"What can I say?" Recognizing Dr. Merk, Julianne scrunched her mouth and shrugged. She was glad he was here. He had the best bedside manner of the current batch of residents.

He patted the table. "Well, hop on up here so I can take a look."

He placed her foot on a pad and gently peeled off the layers of gauze. Bright red blood bubbled through the slit. "You know there are easier ways to get a day off."

Was that a wink? A blush rose up her chest and across her face.

Dr. Merk poured antibacterial rinse over her foot. Wincing, Julianne grabbed the table, closed her eyes, and inhaled sharply. He patted it dry and injected Lidocaine around the edges of the wound.

"That'll numb it so I can stitch you up. It will take a minute or so." He spun around on his stool to the counter and placed equipment onto a tray before spinning back. With the tip of the needle, he tested an area of her foot. "How's that feel?"

"Weird. But it doesn't hurt."

19

Dr. Merk stitched while Julianne counted the ceiling tiles, attempting to create patterns from the dots. Her mind wandered to the previous night. *How could Clay do that to me? Is Bella right? Is there someone else? Oh, God… how am I going to explain this to Momma and Poppy?*

"There, you're all set." His voice startled her back to the present. "Ten stitches. Stay off it as much as possible, ice it, and keep it elevated. Use crutches for the next few days, but you already know all that."

Julianne took Dr. Merk's arm to help her sit up. A wave of dizziness and nausea hit, and she paused on the table. *Wow, so this is how my patients feel after what I would've considered a simple procedure.*

Dr. Merk placed his hand on her arm to steady her. "Take your time." He handed her a slip of paper. "Hydrocodone. You'll probably only need it for a day or two. If your foot starts throbbing, get it above your heart. Trust me. It's not just something we tell our patients—it really works."

Once steady, she slid off the table and took the crutches Shavenda held out for her, suddenly aware of how difficult getting home would be.

Depleted and dejected, Julianne crutched next door to the pharmacy and slumped into a chair to wait. Her thoughts were a tormented jumble. *Please let this all be a bad dream.*

The pharmacist called her name, and she stumbled out of the chair. She hobbled to the checkout and read the patient information while the technician rang her up.

"Do you have any questions for the pharmacist?"

"Uhm, I don't think so."

"If you start to itch while taking this, you can take Benadryl. Do you need some?"

Clay probably took that, too. "Yeah, guess I'd better."

The technician reached over the counter and pulled a box from the display that contained several allergy products. *Ah, yes, spring is here.* He put everything into a bag and handed it to her. Looking directly at her, he flashed a full-dimple smile.

Geez is everyone flirting with me? Do I already have "single" tattooed on my forehead? She responded with a half-effort smile and stuffed the bag into her purse. "Thanks."

Julianne pulled her purse strap over her head and set out for home. Balancing precariously on her crutches, she maneuvered up the few steps to the outer security door and wiggled into her building. She looked up at her door and groaned. That one flight of stairs took a full five minutes to traverse. Once inside, she dropped the crutches and slammed the door.

She hopped to the kitchen sink, dumped the contents of her purse onto the counter, and downed a pain pill with a full glass of water. Standing there staring out the window at what should have been a gorgeous spring day, her vision glazed. Even the daffodils she'd planted in pots on her deck the previous weekend paled. She dug an ice bag from the freezer and heel-hobbled to the living room where she piled pillows onto one end of the couch to elevate her foot. The pain pill soon took effect, dulling her senses, and she drifted into a fitful sleep.

three

*A*t the sound of the rattling doorknob, Julianne bolted upright, almost falling off the couch. Looking around, she struggled to remember why she was in the living room. For a brief second, she thought maybe she'd dreamed last night's events, but the throbbing in her foot pulled her back to reality and told her otherwise.

She grabbed the safety bat lying by the side of the couch. Fighting dizziness, she crept toward the door and held the bat ready to swing. The door slowly opened, its creak echoing off the walls. She swung, stopping within inches of Clay's head.

"Damn it, Clay! I could've killed you with this. What the hell are you doing here?"

"I could ask you the same thing. You're supposed to be at work."

A conversation they had earlier in the week flittered through her mind and suddenly made sense. "At least I understand now why you were so intent on knowing my schedule for the week," Julianne said. "After that little stunt you pulled yesterday, I decided to stay home today." Leaving the door wide open, she hopped to the couch and plopped down.

"What's wrong with your foot? And why is there food all over the floor?"

"None of your damned business," she snarled. "I asked why you're here."

Clay hung back near the door, shuffling from one foot to another. "I came to get a few more things."

"Like what? You took almost everything." Julianne made a grand sweeping gesture, becoming dizzy in the process. The night's binge, on top of the pain pill and no food, took its toll.

Ben's meow shifted the mood and Clayton bent to provide the insisted-upon attention. "Well, Ben, for one," he said, while scratching the fluffy white cat behind the ears. Ben rolled onto his back, batting Clay's hand when he stopped scratching.

"There's no way in hell you're taking that cat!" Julianne spat, as she leaped to grab Ben, forgetting her foot in the process.

Clay lunged to catch her before she could face-plant onto the hardwood floor. "Hey, are you ok?" He helped her to her feet, keeping a protective arm around her.

"Let me go. I'm fine." Julianne struggled out of Clay's arms and crawled back to the couch, more than a bit embarrassed—and a lot angry.

"Ben and Jerry are a pair—you can't split them up," she said, once settled onto the cushions.

"Then I'll take both of 'em. You never liked cats anyway. I was the one that wanted them. Besides, they always liked me better." Hands on his hips, Clay looked determined to win this battle.

"Like hell, you will!" Julianne grimaced, struggling to find a comfortable place for her foot.

Clay let his hands fall to his sides, and his face softened. He took a step in her direction. "Is your foot ok?" he asked, his voice leaking tenderness.

Emotionally and physically exhausted, Julianne's defenses dropped. She sighed heavily, her tensed shoulders relaxing from where they'd scrunched up around her ears.

Julianne shook her head, fighting the tears. "Can you at least tell me why? I had no clue you were so unhappy." She paused and used the back of her hand to wipe the wetness from her face. She looked away, considering what else to say. "Did I do something wrong?"

Clay knelt and continued to pet Ben. "Jules, it's not you. It's me." He rose and asked, "Can I get you anything?"

Julianne chewed her lower lip, looked at him, and shook her head. She contemplated whether she wanted to know. "Is… is there someone else?"

"Jules…" He twisted the toe of his shoe on the floor, head down, hands in his pockets.

She knew. *Guess that's why they say don't ask a question if you don't really want the answer.*

"So that's it. Bella asked me if there was someone else, and I dismissed her. I couldn't imagine you doing that. Huh, you think you know someone…" Dropping her head back on the couch, she stared at the ceiling.

"Jules, I'm…" Clay moved toward her, but stopped at the sight of Julianne holding an open hand toward him, her head cocked to one side.

She let out a long, slow breath and pointed at the door. She didn't need to ask the cliché question, *Are you in love with her?* She already knew that, too.

Clay hovered motionless for a moment. "I'm taking Ben," he said, moving toward Ben.

"Take one more step and I swear I'll…" Julianne whispered through clenched teeth, as she wrapped her hand around the bat.

Clay hesitated.

"You are *not* taking the cats. Period. And leave your keys on the counter. You're done sneaking in here."

Clay put both hands in the air. "Can't we be civil about this?"

"You don't give me the decency to talk to me before sneaking out, and you want *me* to be civil?" Julianne's voice raised an octave. "Seriously? Have you lost your mind?"

She struggled off the couch and glared at her husband. Pointing at the island counter that separated the kitchen from the living room, she said, "Keys."

Clay laid his keys on the counter. "I'm taking Ben." Clay made one more move toward Ben, and Julianne shifted the bat, slapping it in her palm.

"Fine. I'll get him some other time," he said, walking toward the open door.

"In your dreams." Julianne pointed again, raising her voice enough that it echoed in the stairwell. "Out."

Clay shook his head and skulked out.

Julianne hopped to the door and screamed into the hallway, "My attorney will be in touch!" Not that she had one, but she'd seen it in a movie once and it made her feel better.

"Oh, and you can tell your bitch she's welcome to you, you sorry son-of-a-bitch!" She slammed the door, hard, and pressed her back to it. Letting the bat clatter to the floor, she hit the door repeatedly with the side of her fists and screamed.

She limped back and fell onto the couch, angry tears stinging her eyes. Reaching for her pain pills, she took two, curled up, and bawled until sleep overtook her.

four

*J*ulianne opened her eyes to an inky black apartment, seeing nothing but the blinking red glow of a myriad of electronics. Feeling disoriented, she glanced at her clock—10 o'clock. Her stomach rumbled. *Did I eat? Where are the cats? Did the weatherman say snow?* Julianne's stomach lurched and rumbled again, blasting her from her disjointed, medicated thoughts. It didn't matter—she was hungry.

Using one crutch, she half-hopped to the kitchen, weaving through the land mine of scattered groceries on the floor from the previous evening. Retrieving a can of chicken alphabet soup from under the edge of the cabinet, she caught a whiff of sulfuric rot and fought the bile rising in her throat. She dug through the mess. A dozen broken eggs oozed through their cardboard container. "Gross," she said, holding the carton by one end.

Mouth breathing to avoid the smell, she attempted to place it into the trashcan without spilling it back onto the floor. No such luck. Using paper towels, she wiped up the snotty remains. The foil-wrapped meat loaf, meant for their celebration, followed the eggs into the trash.

"Sorry, Marco."

Julianne sighed and looked over the battlefield of spilled groceries. Her throat still raw from screaming, and her eyes puffy from crying, she waved her hand over the mess, as if it might magically disappear. *Later.*

After straightening the microwave on the counter, she searched for an open outlet and plugged it in. She poured the soup into an oversized bowl, set it in the microwave, and pressed "Reheat." She stared at nothing until the ding yanked her back to the present. Wrapping the bowl in oven mitts, she hobbled slowly to the island counter, trying not to spill the hot liquid.

Julianne didn't taste the soup, eating was a means to an end, nothing more. Once done, she stared at the single letter '*a*' stuck to the bottom of her otherwise empty bowl, thinking of all the expletives she could make from it. She jerked her head to try to snap out of the daze.

Rising from the barstool, she maneuvered on her heel, and headed for the sink. She methodically rinsed her bowl and placed it in the dishwasher. Her vision blurred as she again looked over what remained of the mess—*I should clean this.* Everything else faded into the background as her gaze landed on the bottle of pain pills—*Nope, think I'll have two more of those instead.* She gulped them down with a glass of water and dragged herself back to bed.

Sunrays peeked through the blinds. Morning had arrived much too soon for Julianne. Despair draped over her, heavier than her duvet. *Why even bother getting up?*

She lolled in bed until her bladder demanded she get up. Julianne crutched as quickly as possible to the bathroom. Avoiding her reflection when she passed the mirror, she made her way to the kitchen and popped a pack into the coffee maker, desperate for its elixir. *At least he left this.* Halfway through her second cup, she sniffed the air and crinkled her nose. *Geez, I stink. I need a shower*. But her body refused to move. Finally, with a heavy sigh, she pulled herself off the stool and headed for the bathroom. *Maybe it will lift my spirits.*

She stopped cold in the bathroom doorway, dropped her crutches, and groaned. Shattered glass blocked her path to the shower. Dropping to her knees, she used one of the still wet towels to scoop up as much glass as she could before rolling them all together in a clump. She scooped them up and shuffled on her heel to the kitchen. Shaking them over the garbage can, she stopped. *Oh, what the hell, I'll get new ones. Plunk*—she dropped them into the trash along with the glass, on top of the egg snot and meatloaf.

On autopilot, she retrieved the broom and dustpan and swept up the rest of the broken wineglass, depositing it in the bathroom trash, too tired to make it back to the kitchen. She stared at the plops of red blood splotched on pink tile, released a heavy sigh, and left them there.

After wrapping a plastic bag around her foot, she took a scalding hot shower, hoping the gloom threatening to consume her circled and vanished down the drain. As she leaned her head back, and the water poured over her, like a torrential downpour, she realized what she needed: Poppy—he always knew how to make things better.

She dried and put on sweats and a hoodie. Tossing her pain pills into her purse, she headed to the one place where life always made sense.

Julianne parked her Summer Rain blue Prius in front of the tidy row house where she'd spent her childhood. For a moment, she stared at the stained glass door. The tulips planted around the statue of the Virgin Mary in her momma's grotto poked their heads above the mulch. Nearby, daffodils and crocuses swayed in the light spring breeze.

She thought of growing up in The Hill neighborhood: playing in the street until sundown, sleepovers at Bella's, attending church at St. Ambrose surrounded by nuns. Her parents were devout, old-school Catholics. She inhaled deeply, letting the air escape in a slow heavy sigh, feeling the hollow space in her chest. *How will I explain this to my parents? To them, divorce is a sin—couples simply work things out. But how am I supposed to work this out?*

She'd barely made it from the car to the walk before her poppy rushed to help.

"*Tesoro mio,*" he greeted her with his usual flair of affection—using the Italian for "treasure of mine"—wrapping her in his burly arms. "You're hurt, let me help you." He practically carried her up the four steps and inside to the couch.

Simple people, her parents filled their living room with framed pictures of family, both blood and non-blood. They considered everyone who entered their home family and were fiercely loyal.

Safe and comfortable in his arms the dam burst. "Oh, Poppy, Clay ..." Tears drowned her thoughts as she melted into his chest.

"He did this to you?" her poppy asked, pointing to her foot. "No man hurts my *tesoro* and gets away with it."

"What?" her momma shouted from the other room, and hurried in drying her hands on a towel. Her gaze widened, as she looked from the crutches to Julianne's foot, and gasped. "He beat you?"

"No, Momma." Julianne finally took a breath. "Clay left me. I cut my foot on broken glass."

"What? When? Why?" her momma asked, the questions coming in rapid-fire succession, a skill honed from her twenty years as a reporter. A skill Julianne often found charming, except not today.

Her momma moved next to her and stroked her hair. "Don't worry, sweetie, he'll come back." She patted Julianne's thigh. "Are you hungry?" In their house, food was the answer to almost every question.

Julianne looked at her and shook her head, suddenly overwhelmed with extreme exhaustion. "I'm wiped out. Can I take a nap in my room?" she asked, looking from her momma to her poppy.

"Of course, sleep as long as you like. I've got your favorite dish in the fridge." Julianne loved her momma's lasagna, her grandmother's recipe. It made her think of lazy summer days spent alone with her nonna, the two of them making the strips of pasta by hand, preparing for the influx of family for the evening meal.

Her poppy helped her down the long, narrow hallway to her room and over to her bed. "Rest, my *tesoro mio.*" He kissed her cheeks and closed the door without a sound.

Julianne spilled a pain pill into her palm and shook the bottle, taking a quick count of what remained. *Wow, maybe I should slow down a bit.* Not bothering with the covers, she crawled onto her childhood bed and wondered if the world would ever again make sense.

31

The afternoon sunlight slithered through the blinds and teased Julianne awake. Dust danced in the sunbeams, creating an almost misty feel to the air. Stretching, she allowed her gaze to drift around the room, glad her parents had left it as it had been when she'd lived there. Posters of Bon Jovi, Van Halen, Sting, Clint Black, and George Strait—singers she had once idolized—still decorated the walls. Her drill team trophies gleamed on the dresser next to a collection of framed photographs from high school.

Julianne got up and limped over to the dresser. She ran her finger around the edge of one of the pictures, lost in memories. A young girl with a radiant smile and long blond curls pulled into a ponytail smiled at her from the picture. Wrapped in a woolen poncho, she posed on a dusty street surrounded by village children. Behind her, the peaks of Machu Picchu graced the horizon far in the distance.

Julianne rested one hip on the edge of the bed and stared at the photo. *Where did that girl go? When did I lose her? I had such great plans at sixteen. What happened to me?*

The tantalizing aroma of lasagna raised a raucous growl from her stomach. Hunger overtook her grief and she hobbled to the kitchen, holding the photo under her arm. "I'm starving," she announced, setting the photo on the table.

Julianne could always count on her momma having food in the fridge; she had quickly learned the ways of the large Italian family she'd married into and food was a big part of that. Watching her grace and expertise in the kitchen, Julianne found it hard to believe her momma wasn't from Mother Italy—well, except for her distinctive ginger-red hair and pale, freckled Irish features.

Julianne scooted a chair out at the small, metal-legged, laminate table. Her momma removed lasagna from the oven and replaced it with a loaf of garlic bread before taking the seat across from her daughter in the eat-in kitchen. She placed her hand on Julianne's arm, patting it gently.

"What happened? You two seemed so happy when you were here for supper two weeks ago."

Julianne's shoulders dropped and she sucked in a deep breath to ward off the threatening tears. Her chin trembled, and she said, "I thought we were, too, Momma. He moved out while I was at work, no hint or warning. Then he had the gall to sneak in and try to take Ben yesterday. Thankfully, I was home with my injured foot and stopped him."

"He'll come to his senses and come back. Don't worry."

Julianne rested her chin in her hand and lowered her gaze to ponder her momma's statement. "I don't think I want him back," she mumbled.

"Oh, sweetie, don't talk like that. All marriages go through rough patches. Your marriage will be all the stronger for it."

"This is not just some rough patch, Momma," she said, sharper than intended. "He moved out. And …" Julianne dropped her chin to her chest. "He's seeing someone else." She hadn't done anything wrong. Although she wasn't sure why, she felt shame for Clay's actions.

"Given time, that can also be viewed as a rough patch." Her momma spun her wedding ring with her thumb in time to the click-clack of the timer and stared past Julianne's shoulder. The ding of the timer caused her to jump. She walked to the stove and removed the bread. After slicing it, she placed it on a tray alongside a plate of hot lasagna in front of Julianne. Smoothing her apron with her hands, she slid back into her chair. "Look at me and your poppy—we are so happy together. If I'd given up on him when we were young, and he was stupid, you wouldn't be here."

Julianne dug into the lasagna. "Delicious as always, Momma." After a few bites, she glanced up and frowned. "What did you mean by that?"

Nibbling on a slice of garlic bread, her momma remained silent, gazing at Julianne. "I've never told you this, but it seems like now might be a good time." She released the breath she'd been holding. "Your father had an affair early in our marriage, before George was born."

Mid-chew, Julianne stopped and gaped, eyebrows raised. "What?"

"It's true." Her momma shrugged. "I found out and locked him out of our apartment. He left, but came back a few hours later with dear old Father Angelo, God rest his soul," she said, making the sign of the cross. "He cried and begged on his knees for me to forgive him. I prayed every day, for a long time. I wore the polish off two sets of rosary beads. But I finally forgave him and now look at us."

Julianne had trouble reconciling this story with the man she called Poppy, but she had to admit her parents had an enviable relationship. "This is different. Poppy wasn't in love with someone else. He didn't sneak out

34

while your back was turned. What Clay did was reprehensible and I could never trust him again. I simply don't know the person who did this." The knuckles on both hands shone white from squeezing her fists to keep her hands from shaking. "No, Momma, my marriage is over."

Again, her momma smiled and patted her hand. "What is that picture you have there?"

Julianne handed her the photo. "This is from one of the mission trips I took in high school. Remember how excited I was about being a nurse in some foreign land? All those years of Spanish have certainly paid off at work. Now I wonder if perhaps I should've followed that path instead of marrying Clay."

"You're only twenty-six. No path is closed. Give yourself some time before you do anything drastic regarding Clay. After that, if you still feel the same, we'll go see Father Carmichael."

Julianne knew her momma was right; she usually was. She stood and looked from her foot to her plate, and shrugged, grinning at her mother.

"I'll get that." Her momma piled the plates in the sink and returned to hug Julianne. When she tried to pull away, Julianne pulled her tight and rested her head on her momma's shoulder, burrowing in close.

The doorbell chimed, and Bella's bubbly voice called out from the living room. "Jules? I saw your car."

"We're in the kitchen," Julianne and her momma sang out together, Julianne releasing her from their hug.

Bella burst into the kitchen and swept Sibeal into a bear hug. Bella easily had six inches on Sibeal's five-foot three-inch frame. And as her Italian grandmother would say, "She's a sturdy girl. Good birthing hips." Bella put her down, their laughter bouncing off the walls.

"Bella, how are those sweet babies of yours? You really should bring them over more often," Sibeal said, once her feet touched the floor.

Julianne grabbed her crutches. "Let's go out back."

Bella helped Julianne navigate the paver-stone patio and over to the bench swing her momma had insisted on getting the previous spring. It had been a good call—company gravitated there in nice weather.

Once seated, Julianne leaned her head back on the cushion and relaxed for the first time since coming home to Clay's surprise. "You won't believe what my jerk of a husband did yesterday."

"You mean there's something even jerkier than moving out while you were at work?"

"He showed up in the middle of the day and used his key to come in. Scared the crap out of me. I almost clubbed him with our security bat."

"Should have whacked him a good one. He deserved it if you ask me." Bella's infectious laugh usually worked on Julianne, but not this time; she simply stared, looking at nothing. "What the heck did he want?"

"Ben, he wanted Ben. Can you believe it?" Julianne shook her head as silence overtook her, pushing the swing back and forth with her good foot. A single tear ran down her face.

"You were right. There *is* another woman." She looked up and away, her lips pulled downward and her chin quivering in an effort to fight the tears that filled her eyes again. "Damn it! I told myself I wasn't going to give him the satisfaction of making me cry anymore."

Bella reached over and put her arm around her friend, pulling Julianne's head to her shoulder. "It's okay, he can't see you. Cry all you want."

They swung while Julianne cried. Between her sobs, Julianne asked, "Why? Was I really such a bad wife? How he could be that cruel?" She dug in her pocket for a tissue and blew volumes of snot, dropping the soaked tissue on the ground.

"Yuck, here." Bella pulled tissue from her pocket and handed it to Julianne. "Cry it out."

Her sobs gradually reduced to sniffles. Once she'd cried her eyes red and raw, she quieted, looking out at her momma's garden full of yellow, orange, and red daffodils.

Julianne raised her head from Bella's shoulder and shifted her weight so she faced her. "Do you remember those mission trips I took in high school?"

"Sure. You went to Peru, and what, Guatemala, I think it was? You were all gung-ho about saving the world back then."

"I found a picture on my dresser of me in Peru," she said, tilting her head toward the window of her childhood room. "It got me thinking—about what I wanted to do back then. I can't help but wonder about the road not taken, about what happened to those ideas and dreams. Who would I be now if it hadn't been for Clay? Would that passion have faded away on its own?"

"Guess there's only one way to find out. Go, Girl! You gotta take life and run with it. Hey, someone should be having fun beyond diapers," Bella said, snorting. "Look, you always said you wanted to have adventures."

"I can't just drop my life and run off to Peru or wherever."

"And why not? You got no husband, no kids."

"Gee, thanks."

"You know what I mean. You could use some of your vacation to try on this childhood fantasy and see if it still fits."

"Hmmm, I never thought of that. Maybe I could chaperone a teen mission trip, like the ones I went on. I really feel I have something to offer—like give vaccines, or help out in a village that doesn't have a doctor." A tinge of excitement worked its way into Julianne's voice.

She pushed the ground with the toe of her left shoe to restart the stalled swing. "Perhaps I'll talk to Father Carmichael. But I can't decide on anything right now." Julianne stared blankly at her feet, trapped by her thoughts, then shook her head like a wet dog. "Right now, I *just* need to get through right now."

Bella patted Julianne on the thigh. "You'll figure it out. If not now, then later." She hopped off the swing. "I need to head home, told Alessandro I'd only be a few minutes. Saw your car and wanted to check on you."

She leaned over, hugged Julianne, and gave her a peck on the cheek. "Hang in there, sister, you know I love you."

"Love you, too."

As Bella straightened, she asked, "You going back in?"

Julianne looked around at the daffodils. "No, I think I'll sit out here a while. Such a beautiful day. With that predicted snow I want to soak in as much warmth as I can."

"Call me if you get lonely."

Bella left through the side gate. Julianne gave the swing a huge push and lay back. She was staring at the sky poking around the edge of the canopy, listening to the birds, when her poppy ambled up carrying a large fleece blanket.

"May I join you?"

"Always, Poppy."

He eased onto the swing beside her and covered their legs with the blanket. As he placed his arm over her shoulder, Julianne snuggled into his chest. He pulled her in close and kissed her softly on the forehead. "My sweet *tesoro.*"

"How did things go so wrong? How could I have not known?"

"Don't blame yourself for Clay's stupidity. He's obviously a good liar."

"But, how did I miss it? There had to have been signs. I know things have been a bit tense between us lately, but I figured it was because of all the hours I've been putting in working the nightshift."

They swung, their silence interrupted only by the squeak of the swing and the cardinals singing overhead. The birds flitted between the multiple feeders scattered throughout the urban yard. Her momma did her best to fill them during the winter months; her reward was year-round song and splashes of color.

"The night Clay left, I had a big surprise dinner planned for the anniversary of our first date. I went to all this trouble and Marco put a nice spread together. Remember that rolling butcher-block cart we found at the Gypsy Caravan right before we got married?"

"Yes, I had to bring the van so you could get it home."

"Oh yeah, I remember. Well, I set the groceries on the cart, only it wasn't there. The food ended up all over the floor. I thought we'd been robbed."

"Man's a coward. You know I don't believe in divorce, but he doesn't deserve you. I won't tell you what to do, but if he ever comes around here again, I might have to punch him." Her poppy swiped his fist through the air in a mock right-hook and made a goofy face.

"Thanks, I needed a laugh."

They swung until the first hints of twilight appeared, a blazing orange and purple sunset streaking across the sky.

"Stay for supper?"

She shook her head. "I should be getting home. Ben and Jerry will shred the curtains if I don't feed them soon."

"*Tesoro*, you are a strong young woman. I know you hurt now, but you'll get through this and learn new things about yourself. Maybe even discover some things you've forgotten. Momma and I are here for you."

He helped Julianne into the house. She stuck the photo into her purse, hugged her momma, and headed home.

Part Two

Jokob & Keara
...four years earlier

five

By the pre-dawn light of the moon, Keara shivered as she dressed in layers. They'd decided to hike the trails in Estes Park. It was their last week in the Denver area so it was now or never. Getting there early would give them the whole day to explore, but it also meant leaving before the owls hooted.

Always ready should inspiration strike, she packed a sketchpad, pencils, and writing notebook into her backpack. Jokob sorted through cameras and lenses, deliberately selecting the most versatile tools so he could get the most from what he carried. She loved his precise-ness and attention to detail.

She placed their lunch sandwiches in the internal cooler pouch of Jokob's backpack. They'd have dinner in town.

After adding her last water bottle to the net pouch of her own backpack, she said, "Ready, Babe," and swatted his bottom.

"Just one more thing." He inserted his fold-up tripod into his bag and zipped it shut. "Done. You got the food and water?"

Keara grinned. "Check."

They headed out and climbed into their forest green Jeep Wrangler. Jokob had replaced the hardtop with the soft a few weeks earlier, since it was now warm enough during the day to ride with the top off. That was how they preferred to roll.

"I've got the destination plotted into the GPS, a bit under an hour. We should be there before sunrise." He tossed his bag behind his seat and climbed in.

A light mist, not quite a fog, covered the trees and roads. The changing of the seasons from winter to spring in the valley would hide the tops of the mountains, but it was still too dark to see them anyway.

They'd spent the end of winter in and around Denver with the goal of adding snow sunrises and sunsets to their latest book project. It was almost complete, and spring now flirted with making an appearance. Both ready to be rid of the snowshoes and tire chains, they eagerly looked forward to their next stop scheduled for the Washington coastline. It had been years since they'd been out that way and Jokob wanted to attend his friend's wedding in Seattle.

The Jeep's tires crunched on gravel as Jokob steered into the parking area. They climbed out, pulled on backpacks, and flipped open hiking sticks. Jokob did a quick double-check of the map and adjusted his headlamp before starting out on the still dark trail.

He took the lead. They hiked in silence, both content to listen to the pre-dawn forest, rustle of the wind, and crunch of leaves beneath their feet. They remained alert for signs of bear and elk—both could be dangerous if spooked, but made for amazing pictures if seen.

They reached the first outcropping of the mountain and wordlessly agreed to stop here to be ready when the sun began to nibble at the bottoms of the trees.

After dropping their packs, they each removed the tools of their trades—Keara her sketchpad, notebook, and pencils, Jokob his camera and tripod. Always content to be alone together, Keara retrieved a small ground blanket and headed for the edge of the cliff. She loved to sit with her feet dangling into nothingness, imagining herself as a bird, swooping and floating on the air currents.

In the dim, almost-dawn light, Jokob moved slowly, back and forth around the outcropping, aiming and re-aiming his camera, seeking his shots. Once he had the perfect angle, he set up his tripod and attached the camera. He would take at least one hundred pictures at this one location. From that, he might find one or two worth including in a book or show.

As the sun topped the cliffs across the ridge, Keara steadied her pad, waiting for the first sunrays to split the darkness, thirsty for the wonders it would bring. Her drawings and poetry would combine with Jokob's photos to create their planned book, *Sunrise, Sunset—An Adventure in the Wilds of Colorado*. This would be the fifth in a wilderness series began almost two years ago.

Keara carried a small pocket camera used for capturing ideas she might later draw, but Jokob was the true camera artist. What he did with pictures, she did with words and drawings. She focused on the skies where three large birds, condors she guessed, came into view and began circling. As they did, Keara picked up her pencil and wrote.

> *High on thin, crisp air,*
> *Giants float.*
> *The condor ballet takes silent flight.*

Circling and swooping to the other, then away.
Slowly they spin together, ever tightening
*   As they dance on the current.*
One swoops and dives, down,
*   Down to the bottom of the canyon.*
Up again it climbs with empty talon.
It rejoins the condor ballet still in flight.

Buoyed by a lightness in her chest, she took up her charcoal pencil and rough-sketched the mountains, cliffs, and condors in their circling pattern.

Jokob completed his sunrise shots and zoomed in on Keara's intent smile as she focused, her pencil moving furiously across the page. He loved watching her and the energy of her face as she worked. The beauty of her copper-red hair never ceased to amaze him. Today it seemed to glow, the sun's rays glinting off the curls lining the center of her back, held together in a single band at her neck.

"I don't know about you, but I'm hungry," Jokob said, digging through his pack to reach the cooler.

"Hmm, me too."

They moved to a flat rock overlooking the canyon. Jokob laid out the sandwiches. They ate silently and leisurely, enjoying the crisp mountain air, allowing nature to provide their entertainment.

"You about ready to move on?" Jokob loaded his gear, while Keara cleaned all traces of food from their makeshift table.

Keara closed her sketchpad and stowed it in her pack. Loose rocks clinked off the ledge causing her to slip. She slid down the trail on her bottom, pulling the blanket with her. Her scream echoed off the cliffs.

"You okay?" Jokob raced down the trail after her.

"I'm fine. My elbow, however…" She raised it up to show him blood dripping from a nasty looking scrape. "Not so much."

Jokob opened his backpack and removed the first aid kit. "Anything broken?"

"I don't think so."

He used a moist towelette to remove as much rock as possible, applied ointment, and a bandage.

"Thank you. You're my hero." she said. "I should be more careful on these cliffs. I'd hate to fly off the other side." She laughed and rolled up the blanket, stowing it on the outside of her pack.

"That was a delightful spot. Did you see those condors dancing on the currents?" Keara held out her arms, leaning from one side to the other, imitating the birds.

"Magnificent. I got some great shots of them. How 'bout you?"

"I wrote a poem, did a quick drawing, and took a few pictures for later."

Jokob pulled her close for a kiss. His hand lingered on hers, as they started walking, this time with her in the lead.

She reached the Jeep by late afternoon, flicked her hiking sticks closed, and tossed them into the back. Keara swung her pack off and placed it behind her seat. Pulling out a hand towel, she wiped the sweat from her face and neck. Climbing into her seat, she waited for Jokob.

She'd been in the lead on the last leg of the hike, and he'd stopped a hundred yards or so back to take a few more pictures.

She had settled into her seat when Jokob arrived. "Hey slowpoke, what kept you?" She laughed, teasing him.

"Oh, you didn't see that bear you walked right past?"

"What? Where?" Keara jumped out of her seat and planted her boots on the running boards looking over the top of the Jeep. If there was a bear, she wanted to see it. She had only seen two the whole time they'd been in Colorado.

"I'm kidding. There is a bear, but not close. She's on the rise way over there." Jokob pointed to a sparse patch high on the hill overlooking the trail.

Keara cupped her hands above her eyes to block the glare, but it was too far away to see anything. She grabbed her binoculars and tried again. "There! Oh wow. She's got a cub. No, wait, there's another cub. Did you get pictures?"

Jokob laughed. "Yes, I got pictures. You'd think you'd never seen a bear." He settled his gear into the back and climbed behind the wheel. "This was a good day. You ready for dinner?"

"I'm starving. Let's go." Keara snapped her seatbelt, and they were off to Gruber's Inn in Estes Park.

six

Only the slightest hint of light existed when Jokob slid out of bed and dressed, careful not to disturb Keara. He grabbed a breakfast bar, his camera gear, and a medium-weight jacket. He hiked the hundred yards or so to the edge of the cliff near their camper and set up his tripod. The weather report the night before indicated that this would be the pick morning for great sunrise shots. Moving with expert speed, he sighted in a few angles, set up three tripods, and attached cameras. A few more pictures and the project would be ready for the darkroom.

Jokob worked silently and effortlessly, a man comfortable with his craft.

The sun completed its crest of the horizon, Jokob racing between cameras to capture as many views as possible. Intent on the task at hand, Jokob didn't notice he was no longer alone.

Keara waited until the last click of the shutter, before easing up behind her husband. "I thought I'd find you here." She wrapped her arms around his waist and nuzzled her head into his back.

Jokob turned and embraced her. "Good morning, my love. Such a spectacular sunrise. It will make a great addition to the book."

"Hmmmm." Keara slowly licked her lips, catching Jokob's gaze, bright-eyed, with a bewitching grin.

"Here?" Jokob arched an eyebrow.

"Why not? We've got the place to ourselves." She tugged Jokob's hand and led him toward the blanket she'd laid out.

Jokob followed, entranced by her desire. He slowly ran his hand up her thigh, lifting the edge of her skirt. "Hmmm… no panties. Me likes."

They made love on the blanket under the cloudless Colorado sky, oblivious of the circling condors.

Spent, Jokob rolled onto his back and stared at the vast blue overhead. The morning's dew was rapidly burning away. "I think I'd like to live here when we finally decide to settle down."

Keara laughed. "Really? You? Settle down? Hard to imagine you staying in one place."

"Well, someday. When we decide to start a family, this would be the perfect place. Close enough to Denver if we need something. Far enough away to be out of the madness of civilization."

She sat up, her back to Jokob. "What would you say if someday were now?"

He wrapped his arm around her and rested it on an unfettered breast. "You're ready?"

"I don't know that it's so much that *I'm* ready…" Keara peeked over her left shoulder and caught Jokob's eye. She spun around. "As much as it seems to be ready for us."

Jokob scrunched one eyebrow up, one down. "What's ready for us?"

She reached into her skirt pocket and pulled out a small, plastic stick and held out the display for Jokob to see. A large "+" glowed in the middle.

Jokob stared at it for a moment, shaking his head in confusion. He jerked his head up, his eyes flashing with surprise. "Really?"

Keara's grin threatened to break her face. Her head bobbed yes.

Jokob leaped to his feet, still pantless. "Waa Hoo! I'm gonna be a dad!" He yelled to the Colorado sky. He reached down, grabbed Keara's hands, hauling her to her feet and spun her around.

Kneeling down, he ducked his head under her shirt and kissed her belly button. Cupping and bouncing her breasts, he said, "I thought the girls seemed particularly large today."

"Oh, I don't know about that. I'm probably only a few weeks along. I bought the test in town last week."

"I can't believe it." He slowly shook his head. "I love you so much." Jokob raised his gaze to meet Keara's.

"Good thing we're done here so we can head back east." Jokob grabbed his pants and dressed.

"We don't have to go straight home. I thought I'd go see a doctor in Denver and get everything checked out. We can still spend time in Seattle and take a slow journey home. But I want to be there by the third trimester to be with my mom and sisters."

While Jokob worked on storing the photos from the morning's shoot, Keara lounged outside under the camper awning and called obstetricians in Denver, hoping to find one with an immediate opening. She hit pay dirt on the third call.

"Dr. Gourton's office, may I help you?" answered the cheerful receptionist.

"Yes. I need to see an OB. Any chance you have an opening in the next couple days?"

"You're in luck. I had a cancellation for three o'clock today. Can you make that?"

Keara glanced at her watch—two o'clock. Her stomach did a flip-flop as this became more real. "If we leave right now, we can make that. Thank you." She provided her name and phone number, and hung up.

"Jokob?" Keara glanced behind her before jumping up and racing into the camper to find him. "Jokob?" Not seeing him in their tiny living space, she raced to the bedroom, plowing into him just inside the door.

"We gotta go. They can see us at three." She grabbed her purse and threw her phone in it. "We'd better get going if we're going to make it."

"Huh? Now?"

"No, tomorrow. Yes, right now, silly. Come on, come on, come on." She pulled his hand toward the door. "I'll get directions on the way."

seven

A paper gown the nurse provided crinkled and tore in the middle as Keara slipped it on. Climbing onto the exam table, she struggled to pull the back closed, though it provided absolutely no protection from the chill in the air.

"Why do they keep these rooms so frigid? My nips are going to rip right through this gown."

Jokob looked up with a devilish grin. "Really? Ggrr." He moved toward the exam table. The doctor's knock on the door stopped him.

"Good afternoon, I'm Dr. Gourton," she said, shaking Keara's and Jokob's hands. She paused to glance at the laptop screen.

"I see you did a home pregnancy test and it was positive. Well, let's have a look."

She helped Keara lay on the table and lifted her feet into the stirrups. "I'm so sorry, my hands might be a little cold."

Dr. Gourton did a quick pelvic exam, rolled her chair back, and peeled off her gloves. Taking Keara's arm, she helped her sit up. "Congratulations, you are indeed pregnant. I'd say about eight weeks. I'll check the urine sample, too, but you have all the signs. Your intake form indicates that you travel a lot. When was your last well-woman exam?"

"Uh, well," Keara hesitated, "It's been a few years. We're on the road most of the time, with our work.

I'm generally healthy, so don't see the need for many doctor's visits at my age."

"Well, you're here. How 'bout we go ahead and get that out of the way and save you another stop?"

She shot a quick glance at Jokob. "Uh, sure."

"Lay on back down."

Keara again scooted up on the table and slipped her feet back into the stirrups.

Keara focused on Jokob as the doctor performed a thorough pelvic exam. Moving to the top of the table, she examined Keara's breasts. She breezed through the left, but paused and palpated the right breast from multiple angles.

"How long have you had this?" The doctor took Keara's hand and placed it on the right breast.

"What is that? I didn't know that was there." Keara tilted her head toward Jokob, tasting the fear-induced bile already rising in her throat.

"It's probably nothing." The doctor offered her arm and helped Keara sit up. "Sometimes a milk duct becomes inflamed early in pregnancy. But I really don't like the feel of this. Is there a history of breast cancer in your family?"

Keara froze, her breath shallow and ragged. She struggled to swallow the lump that had formed in her throat. "Yes," she squeaked. "My mother's a five-year survivor."

"I don't want to alarm you, but you need to have this checked immediately. I'll have my nurse call my colleague, Dr. Anthony, to see if they can see you right now. Her office is two floors down in this building."

Once the doctor left the room, Keara slid off the table and dressed, unable to look at Jokob.

54

He came to her side and touched her arm. "It's probably just a blocked duct like the doc said. I mean, you're only thirty-one. Isn't that too young?"

Keara squeezed his hand and chewed the inside of her lip while they waited.

The nurse knocked, opened the door, and handed Keara a business card. "Dr. Anthony said for you to come right over and she'll squeeze you in. She's located two floors down. Suite 408."

Keara gathered her purse and jacket. Walking down the two flights of stairs, she clung to Jokob's arm. Opening the door to see several women sitting in the waiting room, memories flooded her. Three huddled with men who held their hands. Two others wore bandanas to cover obviously bald-heads. Another one, sitting off to one side, looked as terrified as Keara felt—back straight as a board, feet placed squarely in front of her, hands on her lap, a vacant glazed stare in her eyes. A young teen girl held the hand of someone Keara assumed was her mother, leaning to one side in a wheelchair, an oxygen tube in her nose.

Unlike the typical hard waiting room chairs, this room had soft, microfiber chairs with deep cushions in muted shades of blue and green. Plush carpeting replaced hard tile, giving the room a warm, homey appeal. Keara had never been in a waiting room designed for comfort. That alone made her anxious.

Keara suppressed a gasp as her throat closed from the thoughts of her mother's journey. *This can't be happening. I'm too young. And, I'm… Oh God, the baby.* She struggled to stay dry-eyed, dreading the worst.

Almost an hour ticked by. Keara jumped when the nurse called out, "Mrs. O'Callaghan."

Jokob looked at Keara and took a deep breath. Rising, he offered her his hand.

Keara gripped it and rose, unsteady, as they followed the nurse to the exam room.

The nurse had her remove her shirt and bra and gave her a soft cloth gown. *At least it's warm.*

Dr. Anthony came in almost immediately. "Good afternoon. I'm so sorry for the wait," she said, shaking their hands. "I spoke with Dr. Gourton. She says you're about eight weeks pregnant and that she found a mass during your exam. Your mother is a breast cancer survivor? Do you know what kind?"

Keara tucked her chin in and shook her head. "I'm sorry, I don't know. She completed treatments about five years ago. She's fine now, as far as I know."

"With any luck this mass will be nothing to worry about. However, with your family history we can't take chances. Lie on back."

With expert fingers, Dr. Anthony palpated Keara's right breast. She scrunched her face in deep concentration. "Can you roll onto your right side?"

Keara did as asked, unable to read Dr. Anthony's face. Her mind raced to thoughts of her mother's cancer, concocting a worse than worse-case scenario. Her breath came in shallow bursts of ragged gulps.

The doctor examined her again before asking, "Your left side now, please." Once more, her fingers palpated Keara's breast, but her stoicism cracked. She stepped back from the table and leveled her gaze at Keara. "I really wish I could tell you I thought this was nothing. I would like to do a needle biopsy. That will tell me whether we need a full biopsy. Is it OK to proceed with that?"

"Is that safe? I mean, for the baby?"

"Absolutely."

Unconvinced, Keara looked at Jokob. His gaze fixed on her, he replied with an almost imperceptible nod. "Okay, let's get this done now."

"I'll have my nurse prep you and I'll be back in a few minutes."

The nurse came in carrying a small tray containing a needle, cleaning solution, and a slide kit. She bathed Keara's breast with Betadine solution. "The doctor will be right in," she said, and left the room.

Keara stared at the ceiling. "Would you hold my hand?"

"Sure, babe." He faced her, smiling into her eyes. He leaned over to kiss her and the door opened.

The nurse entered and said, "Mr. O'Callaghan, could I get you to sit over there?" She pointed at a chair on the other side of the room.

Dr. Anthony slipped on her gloves. "This shouldn't hurt. We use a very thin needle, much thinner than those used for shots."

She pulled the rolling tray to her side and adjusted the overhead light. "Could you place your right arm over your head? Now, take a deep breath, and let it out slowly."

As Keara breathed out, the doctor inserted the needle. She pulled back on the syringe and looked at it. She did this three times, in different locations.

"I'm not getting fluid. When that happens, I like to go ahead and do a Core Needle Biopsy. It hurts a bit, but it's more accurate. I will need to numb your breast. Is that okay?"

Keara swallowed, but agreed, and the doctor drew a syringe full of local anesthetic.

"This will take about five minutes to fully numb you. I'll be back to proceed."

When the door clicked shut, Keara curled into a ball and burst into tears. "This is bad. I feel it."

Jokob wrapped his arms around her and simply held her, letting her cry out her fear. By the time the doctor and nurse returned, she had calmed and lay back down.

"This is the needle I use," she said, holding it up for Keara to see. "It's larger, but you shouldn't feel anything other than pressure. Go ahead and put your arm up again and take a deep breath in and let it out, like before."

The doctor took four samples from different angles, using her hands to palpate the mass for position.

When she was finished, she tossed her gloves through the slot under the sink and helped Keara sit up. "I'll get the samples sent to the lab immediately. It will be a few days before we have the results, and I know those days will be nerve-racking." Placing her hands on Keara's, she looked directly into her eyes. Her tone softened. "I also know it does no good for me to tell you to try and not worry. But I'll say it anyway. Try to find something to distract you. I will call as soon as I know something."

eight

Keara squirmed in her lounger under the camper awning attempting to read a new novel she'd picked up in town. After reading the same paragraph three times, she laid it on her chest and closed her eyes. Her phone rang and she jerked upright. Pulling it from her pocket, she looked at the caller ID and froze, letting it ring. Once, twice, she picked up after the third.

"Hel—" her voice caught. "Hello?"

"Mrs. O'Callaghan?"

"Yes."

"This is Dr. Anthony's office. The doctor would like you to come to the office this afternoon to go over your test results. Can you make one o'clock?"

"Can't I get the results over the phone?"

"I'm sorry. It's against our policy to discuss results over the phone. The doctor wants to see you."

Keara's voice thinned to a squeak. "I'll be there." She hung up and stared into space.

"Was that the doctor's office?" Jokob's voice jarred her back to reality.

"They want to see me at one." She looked up at him, her lower lip quivering. "This… this… If it was nothing, they would have told me over the phone." The words spilled out with a rush of tears.

Jokob knelt by her lounger. "It still could be nothing, or maybe it's just a minor thing. Let's not get all worked up about it until we know something for sure."

He laid his head in her lap. Numb, she stroked his hair, her tear-blurry eyes turning the mountains in the distance into a Salvador Dali painting.

"Mrs. O'Callaghan."

The nurse held open the door for Keara and Jokob. "This way," she said, leading them to Dr. Anthony's office.

Three soft, blue-green micro-fibered chairs formed a semi-circle on one side of the desk. Keara allowed her knees to collapse her into one of them.

Jokob paced, glancing at the various diplomas and awards. "Washington University School of Medicine," he said to Keara, who didn't acknowledge him.

A credenza behind the massive oak desk contained photos of three children: two boys and a girl, all under the age of five.

"They're not so young anymore," Dr. Anthony said, as she walked in. "They are all teenagers now. I keep that picture to remind me of when they were still young and sweet." Dr. Anthony laughed a bit and shook their hands. She pulled up one of the three chairs, instead of sitting behind the desk.

She pointed at the third chair. "Jokob, won't you join us?"

Smoothing her skirt, she remained quiet for a moment. "There's never an easy way to say this. You have cancer. It's the HER2 type, which is estrogen activated and aggressive. The pregnancy caused it to grow rapidly. Before I outline a treatment plan, we need to do a full body scan to determine if the cancer is still local or whether it's spread."

Keara heard nothing past the word cancer. She squeezed Jokob's hand harder and harder. The room spun as she struggled to hold on to the world as she knew it.

"I'm very sorry to—"

Keara interrupted her. "Stop. Wait. I need. I can't breathe." She drew deep gulps of air through her nose, pulling her head backward. "I can't breathe."

"Bend over, and put your head between your knees," Dr. Anthony advised.

Keara wrapped her arms under her legs. Once she was breathing normally, she sat up and glared at the doctor.

"I'm sorry, but your best chance of surviving is to terminate the pregnancy."

"What? No." Keara's gaze darted between the doctor and Jokob. "I won't do that." She jumped up and paced. "I simply won't. You'll have to find another way."

Jokob grabbed her hand and rose, pulling her close. "Sweetheart, please hear the doctor out. I want this baby as much as you do, but I want you more."

Keara pulled away from his arms, grabbed the doorknob, and ran from the room.

Jokob looked at the doctor. "Schedule the next test. I'll talk to her."

She handed him a card. "It's already scheduled. Go now to building number three, next door. The sooner we know if it's spread, the sooner treatment can begin. I usually get the results in twenty-four to forty-eight hours, but I don't want to wait." She shook her head. "I plan to read the results as soon as they call, so just come back here."

Jokob raced out of the room to find Keara.

He found her in a corner at the far end of the hallway, squatting with her back against the wall, arms wound tightly around her knees, head down, and sobs racking her. He slid down next to her and pulled her into his lap, like he might a child.

"I won't do it."

"I know, my love. We'll talk later, after the next test."

Keara placed her hand over that of the technician. "Will this hurt my baby?" she asked, as he prepared to inject the dye that would cause any cancerous lesions to light up.

"Not that I know of."

The answer didn't help her feel any more comfortable. As she listened to the hum of the PET scan, she tried to go deep into her mind, to find the space where she wrote poetry. All that came to her were torturous verses of death and decay.

When the test was complete, she asked the technician, "Did you see anything?"

The technician diverted his eyes, hesitating. "I'm not allowed to... I'm sorry." He caught her gaze briefly before looking away again. "You'll need to talk to your doctor. The order states that you're to go back to her office and wait."

But Keara saw in his eyes what he couldn't say.

As soon as they arrived, the nurse ushered them straight into the doctor's office. Keara gripped the chair arms, eyes closed. Jokob stood behind her, softly rubbing her shoulders.

When the doctor arrived, she carried a laptop with her. She again took one of the chairs on their side of the desk. When Keara didn't look up, or acknowledge that anyone had entered the room, Dr. Anthony reached out and placed a hand on Keara's arm.

"I know this is difficult. I don't just say that as a doctor. I say that as a woman who has also had breast cancer."

Keara slowly raised her head, red-rimmed eyes burning. She softened her brow. "I'm sorry."

"They found mine shortly after my third child was born. It's because of my own experience that I became an oncologist. Once I got the all-clear, I changed specialties. Having sat where you're sitting makes me a better doctor."

"Thank you for telling me."

"I don't usually send a patient for a PET scan so quickly, but I don't usually see a patient with a mass the size of yours that doesn't collapse with needle aspiration."

The doctor opened her laptop and set it on the desk, screen open toward them. She brought up a colorful picture of Keara's abdominal area. It might have been considered pretty if it wasn't so deadly. "I'm afraid the news I have for you isn't good. You see this area here?" she asked, circling an area with her finger. "That's your liver. And that," she said, pointing to a bright blue spot, "that, is a lesion. The cancer is already stage four, and it's in your liver and spine."

"I thought my back pain was due to the pregnancy." Keara chewed her thumbnail; her right eye twitched.

"I'm afraid not." The doctor closed the laptop. "This is very serious and we need to begin treatment right away. Since it's already metastasized, surgery is not an option. Instead, we'll do targeted radiation and chemotherapy."

"But won't those hurt the baby?"

"There are studies indicating that cancer treatments after the first trimester don't harm the fetus."

"Then we'll wait a month to start treatment." Keara said, her voice bright with hope.

"We can't. This type of cancer is ultra aggressive. Waiting a month could be a death sentence."

The room became silent, except for the raindrops slamming against the window.

"What are my chances? How long do I have? With treatment… and without?" Keara's voice was steady and low-pitched, her shoulders pulled back, head high.

"Without treatment, a few months… maybe. With treatment, you have a better than fifty-fifty chance of beating this and going on to live a long life. I've had patients worse off than you survive. I've also had patients with a much better prognosis not make it. A lot depends on you. I have to advise you again that your best hope for survival is to terminate the pregnancy. You need all your resources to fight this. Diverting anything to growing a fetus reduces your odds. At eight weeks of gestation there is a high likelihood the baby will either not survive the treatment or have serious deformities."

"I understand…but my answer is still no. If we don't do treatment, is there any chance I could live long enough for my baby to be born?"

"Keara, you can't be serious." Jokob jerked to his feet. "There's no way I'm going to let you skip treatment. Once you beat this, we can try for another baby."

Keara scowled at Jokob and cocked her head to one side, a frown etching her brow. She remained silent for a moment before raising her eyebrows. "*Let* me? You won't *let* me? Since when has that ever been a part of our relationship? I love you, but I will do what I think is best."

She focused her attention on the doctor. "One last question. Is there any chance the baby could survive the treatment? Have there been cases?"

"Yes, but as I mentioned, they have been when treatment started much later in the pregnancy. This early, there are too many systems that haven't fully formed. The drug cocktail used to fight stage four cancer is extremely toxic. We'll be lucky if you survive, much less an undeveloped fetus."

Keara rose and held out her hand. "Doctor Anthony, thank you so much. But it's time for me to head back to Cape Cod and my family."

Dr. Anthony let her breath out in a rush and stood. "I understand. One of my colleagues recently moved back to Cape Cod to be closer to family." She walked around her desk and opened a drawer. Handing a card to Keara, she said, "She's recently gone into practice with Dr. Bart Henry. She was my doctor during my treatment. She will take excellent care of you."

Keara lifted one side of her mouth into a lopsided smile. "Dr. Henry was my mother's doctor."

Part Three

Julianne

nine

"So have you seen a lawyer yet? It's been three months." Bella queried Julianne between bites of salad in the hospital cafeteria.

Bella had been in the neighborhood, and Julianne was delighted to be able to get away for a quick lunch. St. Louis Children's Hospital was like a small self-contained city, which made getting out for lunch virtually impossible. Lunch usually consisted of a quick bite at the nurses' station, eaten between patient calls. The cafeteria bustled with doctors, nurses, and patient's families. Some took their trays to tables; others took their food to go.

"No, but Momma said I should talk to Father Carmichael. I don't really know how all this is supposed to work, but she said since there are no children and given the circumstances, I might be able to have the marriage annulled." Julianne picked at her salad, little of it actually making it into her mouth. She hoped Bella hadn't noticed how thin she'd become. The last thing she needed was her nagging her about it.

"So what's new in your life?" Julianne asked, hoping to shift the subject away from her own mess.

"Isabella is walking now. You've got to come over and see her and Nicky. They miss their Auntie Jules."

"It would be nice to chill with the wee ones. My four-day rotation ends Wednesday, so I'm off through Sunday. How about Saturday?"

The best friends didn't see each other as much as they'd like since Julianne and Clay moved to the Central West End to be closer to their work. Julianne loved being able to walk or bike to work on nice days. And she loved living two blocks from Forest Park and the St. Louis Zoo. Although not far from The Hill neighborhood where they'd grown up, and where Bella still lived, it was no longer next door.

"Good. I'll thaw out some pork steaks and brats for Alessandro to grill." His name slid off her tongue like butter.

Julianne smiled at how Bella said his name—delicious and sexy—wishing to know that feeling. Even after five years of marriage, Bella refused to call him anything other than his given name, knowing she could turn him on by simply saying it, smiling demurely, and looking up at him from under lush, dark lashes. All their friends simply called him Alex. Both from second-generation immigrant families with deep ties to Italy, they spoke fluent Italian.

"Uh, I was thinking perhaps I could invite Steve from work. He's new in town, and—"

Julianne snapped, "If you do, I'll... if I get there and he's there, I'll leave and never speak to you again." She dropped her fork into her salad, glowering at her friend. "It's too soon for me to date. Besides, I'm not even single again yet."

"Okay, okay, don't get your panties all in a knot."

Julianne glanced at her pendant watch. "Crap, I'm gonna be late getting back to work." She hugged Bella. "See you Saturday. Remember, just us." She pointed her finger at Bella to emphasize her intention, turned, and raced off, power walking toward the elevator.

When her shift was over, Julianne stopped at Marco's for takeout. She'd been doing this a lot. Cooking for one was too depressing. Walking through the door, she spied an impeccably dressed, leggy blonde checking out. The woman looked over and visibly flinched, turning her head away. Julianne suspected who she was, but never expected the woman to come over and start talking to her.

"Are you Jules? May I call you Jules?"

Julianne flashed a dirty look at this woman who had disgustingly perfect china-smooth skin, long blond hair with coiffed waves in all the right places, and legs that started at the floor and seemed to have no end. "If you're who I think you are, then no you may *not* call me Jules. How dare you even speak to me?" Julianne shook her head, her face clenched in anger.

"I'm sorry." The woman hung her head, allowing her hair to hide her face. "But I need to try and explain. I know what you must think of me, but you don't know the whole story. Please, I only need a few minutes."

Curiosity got the better of her, and Julianne pointed to a secluded corner of the market. "You've got two minutes," she said, once they were out of traffic. She checked the time, shifted her weight onto one hip, and crossed her arms over her chest. She tapped one foot up and down, like she was keeping time to a song.

The woman took a deep breath, and said, "My name is Michelle. I know you think I'm a horrible person, but

Clayton lied to me, too. He told me he was recently divorced. I didn't know he was still married until Gary let it slip a couple of weeks ago. I would never have been with him if I'd known. I'm not *that* woman."

Julianne noticed the telltale bags peeking through the expertly applied makeup, the reddened eye rims. The pleading look on Michelle's face told Julianne it was the truth. A lump formed in her throat, but she managed to squeak out, "How could you not have known he was married? Didn't you see the tan line from his ring? Weren't you curious as to why he couldn't see you at night? Or go anywhere public with you?" Julianne rolled her eyes up to the ceiling and shook her head. She pursed her mouth together, chewing her lower lip.

"Like I said, he told me he was recently divorced. I figured the tan line was because it was so recent. And by the way, didn't *you* wonder where he was all those nights he spent with me?" the woman unexpectedly snapped back.

Feeling like she'd been slapped, Julianne gasped as the reality finally hit her. "That son-of-a-bitch."

She paused to gain control of emotions threatening to run wild. "That little sneak had it all figured out. I'm a nurse, and switched to the night shift about six months ago." She uncrossed her arms as the fight left her.

"I'm really, truly sorry. I should have known something wasn't right when he never took me to his apartment. He said he had a slob for a roommate and didn't like to invite people over. We'd been dating a few months when I learned I was pregnant. That's when he decided to move in with me."

The room spun. A static roar filled her head, and she swallowed the urge to throw up. Julianne reached for a shelf to steady her wobbly legs.

"Are you OK? You're white as a sheet." Michelle reached out her hand.

"You're… " Julianne struggled to choke out the words that felt like crispy paper in her tacky dry mouth. "Pregnant?"

"I was." Michelle paused, dabbing her nose with tissue. "When I found out he'd lied, I… I didn't know what to do. But I realized I couldn't raise a child alone, and never wanted anything to do with that liar again. I simply didn't want him in my life, in any way. So I made the painful decision to terminate the pregnancy."

Michelle turned away and blew her nose before turning back. "I kicked him out of my apartment, told him things I won't repeat in polite company. I can't believe I let myself fall for his lies." Her gaze pleaded for understanding, as she stole a peek up at Julianne, but quickly ducked her head back down.

Julianne stared at Michelle for a moment, and realized they were the same—Clay had lied to and cheated on both of them. She felt sorry for this poor woman, doing what she did, and admired her courage in speaking to her. She put her hand on the woman's forearm. "Thank you. I'm sorry for what he did to you. I… I… I need to go."

Julianne rushed out the door, completely forgetting she'd gone in to get supper.

Home and tired after her surprise encounter with Michelle, Julianne dissolved into tears as soon as the door shut. *He lied to both of us. Who the hell is this man?* She stomped into the kitchen and poured herself a glass from an open bottle of Merlot. She drank it in a gulp, poured another, and headed for the couch.

She'd barely settled back when the doorbell rang. She clicked pause on the TV DVR and peeked through the peephole. "Crap!"

She growled.

"What?" she demanded, making no attempt to keep the irritation from her voice. Allowing the door to crack open, held by the security chain, she blocked the entrance.

"Can I come in?"

"Why in the name of all that is holy should I let you in?"

"Please, Jules, it's important."

Julianne grudgingly slammed the door and removed the chain. She left it sitting ajar and moved away. "You have a lot of nerve coming here."

"Look, can we talk?" Clay paced in circles around the kitchen island, running his hands through his hair.

"And just why would I want to talk? We have nothing to talk about. You made sure of that by cheating and sneaking out. You made your choice." Julianne planted her feet, hands on her hips, making little snorting sounds through her nose.

"Jules, I'm really sorry for that. It was mean and unfair. I was confused and didn't know what else to do. I didn't think I could go through with it while looking at you."

Julianne was silent. Clay paced, rubbing the palm of his hand over the stubble of beard from a few days growth. His usually perfect auburn hair appeared

74

disheveled, as if he'd recently awakened and had forgotten to brush it... or wash it for that matter.

Clay motioned to Julianne's glass of wine and the bottle. "OK if I pour myself one?"

When she didn't answer, he helped himself to a glass and downed it, like a shot of whiskey. He poured another and gulped it, too, draining the bottle.

Julianne crossed her arms over her chest and tapped her foot. "I'm waiting."

His back to her, hands on the bar, he said, "Sweetie, I want to move back home. I made a huge mistake, and I'm sorry."

He spun around and moved toward her, gazing at her with glacial blue eyes made even more luminous by the hint of blood-shot red around the edges. "I know I hurt you and I want to spend the rest of my life making it up to you. Please forgive me." He reached out and touched her cheek with the backs of his fingertips.

Julianne jumped back, like she'd been burned. "Stop it!" She sputtered, "I can't. I loved you, and you... you..." Tears threatened, but she wasn't going to give him the satisfaction of seeing her cry. She bit her lip and pulled her arms tightly across her chest, hugging herself.

"I thought things would be different," he explained, again running his hands through his hair, visibly upset. "I thought I was in love. She was pregnant, and I mistook my feelings about being a father as love for her. But Jules, she had an abortion without even talking to me first."

Julianne swung around and slapped Clay across his left cheek. "I met Michelle today. Seemed like a nice woman. A little too china-doll perfect, but nice. She told me all about your lies to her."

75

Clay had a deer-in-the-headlights look.

"Was she the first? Or just the first that caught you?"

Clay held his reddening cheek. He tilted his head down and looked at her from under his lashes, but said nothing.

"Oh my gawd, you are some piece of work. Get out," she screamed, and shoved his chest full force. Clay stumbled backward, dropping his glass of wine, spraying Merlot-red and glass across the floor and walls of the kitchen.

"Get out! Get out! How dare you come here, ask my forgiveness and tell me this bullshit!" Julianne grabbed Clay by the arm and dragged him toward the door. She shoved him out, slamming the door so hard her framed picture of the Telluride Bluegrass Festival fell, shattering when it hit the floor, picture glass mixing with wine glass shards and wine.

She turned and stubbed her toe on the box of stray items she'd been collecting for him. She stooped and grabbed the box, opened the door and threw it out after him. "Do NOT come back here. Ever. For any reason," she screamed, and slammed the door again.

Julianne slid her back down the door to the floor. She stared at her trembling hands. Clay gone, she now allowed herself to release the tears she'd been struggling to hold. *How could he do this?* Her shock and anger was as fresh and painful as they'd been three months earlier when he'd snuck out. *How on earth could my husband impregnate another woman? Cheating was bad enough, but this?"*

Sniffling, Julianne slowly maneuvered around the blades of glass to her phone. "Momma, could you call Father Carmichael for me? It's time."

ten

Julianne entered St. Ambrose Church through the ornately carved wooden doors and made straight for the prayer candles. She lifted the long match and lit a candle. Even though the church was empty, she chose the last pew and knelt to pray. *I've failed. Failed at the one thing that matters most in the eyes of God—my marriage. What did I do wrong?*

The past three months had been a roller coaster ride of emotions, but meeting Michelle and learning about the baby had been the last straw. She needed out of this marriage, and her mother had convinced her to come see the family priest. Although she would have to get a legal divorce, too, she wanted an annulment. Although not a strictly practicing Catholic, some things ran deeper in her blood, and sanctity of marriage was one of those things. So she didn't just want an annulment, she needed one.

The creak of the rectory door announced the arrival of Father Carmichael, the priest who had both baptized her and officiated at the very wedding she now wished to dissolve.

"Father Carmichael. Thank you so much for seeing me."

The elderly priest reached out and took one of her hands between his. "My dear child, of course. Your blessed mother told me a little of your plight. Let's go into my office." He placed his arm around her shoulder, led her down the hall, and ushered her into his neatly appointed office: a small, serviceable desk, an ornately carved statue of Jesus behind it, and walls lined with shelves overflowing with books.

He closed the door without a sound and motioned for her to take one of the Chippendale style upholstered wingback chairs, most likely donated by a wealthy parishioner since they looked out of place in the otherwise simple, masculine room. He took the other.

"Now, tell me child, what can I do for you?"

"Momma told you what has happened in my marriage?"

"She did. You feel your marriage is irretrievably broken?"

"Father." Julianne stifled a sob. "I believe in marriage. I would never seek an annulment and divorce lightly. But, Father, Clayton didn't just cheat on me. He moved out while I was at work when the woman he was seeing became pregnant."

The floodgate broke and Julianne couldn't speak through her sobs. The priest handed her a box of tissue and waited.

"Please, continue."

"I learned that he also lied to her, making her believe he was recently divorced. When she found out about his lies, she had an abortion. She made him move out of her apartment."

"Those are weighty charges indeed. Is it possible, with the right counseling, you could find it in your heart to forgive him? Would he be willing to try?"

Julianne reflected on the priest's words. She looked around his office, the same office where she and Clay had received their pre-marital counseling.

"Father, I have given this a great deal of thought and prayer. Clay's actions speak volumes about his character.

He broke our sacred vows and caused another to commit a horrible sin. And this woman wasn't the first. I simply don't see how I can commit myself to continuing a life with someone who places so little value in me." She paused and searched the priest's eyes. "These things make it impossible to recover the marriage. I want an annulment."

"I hear your words, my dear," he said, patting her hand. "And I feel your heart. I am always deeply saddened when the marriage of a parishioner is lost, but in spite of the teachings of the church, there are times when it's the right thing. You were married for three years and you have no children?"

"Yes."

Father Carmichael reached for a file on his desk and withdrew a single form. "I've known you your entire life. I christened you in this very church. I do not believe you would seek this without a great deal of contemplation. I believe you have grounds for an annulment. It may take up to two years to be approved and it will require Clayton to sign it also. Will he?"

"He may need a little encouragement from you."

"I'm happy to do that. Also, you'll need two witnesses, preferably not related to you."

"Bella and Alex."

"Ah, yes, delightful couple."

"Thank you, Father." Julianne bowed her head, again feeling shame she didn't fully comprehend. She'd done nothing wrong. And yet, feel shame she did.

Once she signed the paper, Julianne breathed a sigh of relief. "Father, there's something else I would like to seek your counsel on… if you have a few minutes."

"Oh course, dear."

"I've been thinking about the mission work I performed as a teen. I was wondering what connections you have where I might be able to use my training as a nurse? Oh, and my fluent Spanish."

Father Carmichael's knees crackled, as he stood, and shuffled to a small file cabinet tucked between bookshelves. He pulled a brochure from a file in the top drawer and handed it to Julianne. "There are a few, but the one that immediately jumps to mind is in Roatan, Honduras. They desperately need doctors and nurses at the Lady of the Tides Orphanage and Hospital. They ask that volunteers stay at least two weeks but prefer longer if possible. I've been there myself many times and they do good work. There is never enough time, people, or money to meet the inexhaustible need. The accommodations are modest mind you, but clean. I can make contact with them for you if you wish."

"Thank you, Father. I'm not sure I'm quite ready to commit yet, but wanted to know what might fit and determine any prep work I'd need in order to go."

"Well, you could start by getting vaccines. There are several you should get—Hep A and B, which you've probably already had as a nurse, Typhoid, Yellow Fever, and Rabies—you'll want to get all of these well in advance of travel. And check our government's travel board for others."

"That's a great idea. I could get those out of the way now while I plan vacation time."

Julianne accepted a hug from her lifelong priest. "Thank you."

eleven

*A*untie Jules!" Nicky pounced before the door closed and almost knocked Julianne off her feet. Isabella wrapped herself around Julianne's leg. Peanut, their tan and black Yorki-poo, barked, ran in circles, and danced on her hind legs to announce her arrival.

Julianne knelt to hug three-year-old Nicky. "You look more like your daddy every day." She picked up Isabella, the spitting image of Bella. Absolute delights, Julianne loved nothing more than to spend time with them. It had been far too long.

Alex waved from the kitchen. "Come on in. Bella's out back getting things put together."

Julianne placed Isabella on the floor. "I brought wine coolers and brownies. Where would you like them?"

"There's a cooler with ice on the deck. Go on out."

She tried to extricate herself from the one-year-old who'd attached herself to a leg. Failing, she held up a bag. "Ok kids, who wants to help Auntie Jules carry this?"

"Me! Me!" Nicky jumped up and down, vying for Julianne's attention.

Julianne handed him the bag with the brownies. "Here you go. Take this to your daddy."

Nicky ran off, clearly delighted to be helping.

She looked down again at the tiny cherub using her foot as a chair. "On second thought, Alex, I'll let you get the drinks. I'm a little tied up right now." She bent over, swept Isabella into her arms, and up into the air. "Wheeeee."

"Moh." Isabella squealed and giggled. "Gin."

Julianne tossed her again, caught her, and spun in a circle. The giggles echoed off the walls.

"Let's go see what Mommy's doing." She took both of Isabella's hands and helped her out to the yard, one baby step at a time.

They found Bella setting out plates on the picnic table. "Is this new?" Julianne asked, brushing her hand across the wooden table.

Bella looked up and laughed. "Heya girlfriend. I see you found my rug rat. Yes, Alessandro finished putting it together this morning."

"She's grown so much since I saw her last." Julianne played with Isabella's chock of curls, which were starting to thicken and lengthen. Her olive complexion, dark moon-shaped eyes, and luscious long lashes added to her beauty.

"What can I do to help?"

"You're doing it. Keep those little hands out of the grill and we're set. "

Julianne huddled to Bella's side and whispered. "So, before we sit down, I have to tell you something. I met her. Clay's *her*. You won't believe this, but he lied to her too. She thought he was divorced, he got her pregn—"

"What the hell? She's pregnant?" Bella interrupted. "That's insane Jules. How on earth did he think he could get away with that shit?"

"She *was* pregnant. When she found out he'd lied about everything, she got an abortion. And that's not all. The same day I met her, Clay showed up at my door, drunk. He was crying and saying he'd made a mistake and he wanted to come back home. Can you believe that? Come home? After what he did? No way."

"You said it, girlfriend."

Julianne looked at the table and counted six settings. She frowned and gave Bella a scowl. "Uh, who's the sixth?"

"Don't get mad. Alessandro invited a work buddy."

"What?" She stomped her foot. "I told you no one else."

"I know, and I didn't invite Steve, but I can't control what Alessandro does. He invited some guy from work. But you're here now, so please stay. You don't have to marry the guy, just eat with him."

Julianne tilted her head, a hand on her hip. "Oh, all right, damn it. I'm going to go grab a wine cooler."

She settled Isabella on the grass and headed through the screen curtain. Rounding the corner to the living room, she ran headlong into a brick-wall-chest carrying beer and wine coolers.

"Whoa, I'm sorry, I didn't see you. You okay?" He reached out to steady her.

Julianne grabbed the offered arm, and gaped at his chiseled, actor-good-looking features. Once steady on her feet, she extended out her hand. "Hi. I'm Julianne. You must be Alex's friend?"

"Yeah, hi, Rick." His head remained pointed straight ahead.

Julianne squirmed as his eyes traced her up and down.

"Yeah, we work together. So... " Rick stayed a bit too long with the handshake.

"I heard." In spite of her initial resistance at him being there, Julianne found herself staring back. *Tall, good looking, nice smile. Hmmm… maybe this won't be so bad after all.* "I was heading in to grab the drinks, but I guess you beat me to it."

Julianne caught a glimpse of Bella and Alex shooting each other a thumbs-up through the kitchen window.

"Bella, look who I ran into in the doorway. Literally." Julianne came through the screen-flap doorway into the backward, Rick fast on her heels. She stopped short to avoid tumbling over Isabella crawling on the deck, and he slammed right into her back.

"Yeah, we gotta stop meeting like this." Rick laughed as he helped Julianne stabilize herself by wrapping his arms around her waist, a six-pack in one hand.

Julianne stiffened and pried herself free. Turning, she flashed him a fake-smile. "Thanks, I'm good." She plucked a wine cooler from one of the six-packs and strolled to the table to help Bella.

"Ready to cook," Alex announced, stepping onto the deck. After lighting the burners, Alex popped back inside to grab the brats and pork steaks marinating in his secret sauce. "The meat comes from Springs Farm—all humanely raised and organic. It tastes so much better than that corporate-complex meat from the grocery."

The meat sizzled as Alex arranged it on the grill. He closed the lid and bent to the ice chest for a beer.

"Hey Rick, have you ever tried a Schlafly Raspberry Hefe-weizen? It's their summer seasonal. Great picnic beer. I picked these up this week. I'm somewhat of a connoisseur if I do say so myself. Microbrew has so much more character than that mass-produced swill. I'll even have a batch of my own ready to drink in a month or two." He handed one to Rick.

"Hmmm, you're right. So…"

Alex and Rick mingled at the grill making small talk while Bella and Julianne finished setting the table, taking turns keeping Isabella's octopus fingers away from danger. Nicky and Peanut chased each other around the yard, Nicky laughing, and Peanut fake growling and barking.

Back in the kitchen, Bella set corn on the cob, baked beans, and slaw on the pass-through window ledge. "Rick," she called out. "Make yourself useful."

Rick took the items to the table.

"Meat's ready." Alex brought two plates of meat and placed them in the middle of the table. He cut brats into tiny pieces, arranging them on Isabella's high chair table, adding a tiny plop of beans. "Come here, monkey." He picked her up and slid her into place.

Bella cut up bites of brats and pork steak for Nicky, and got him settled in his booster seat. She put the rest on her plate. "Come on. Mangia! Mangia! Grab some food and eat," she said to Rick and Julianne.

Rick climbed onto the seat across from Julianne. "Yeah, so what do you do?"

"I'm a nurse at Children's," she answered between bites.

"Yeah, I'm an IRS auditor. Travel a lot. Yeah, I'm usually in the office one day a week and home on weekends. Otherwise, I'm on the road. So…"

Julianne was surprised to find that although they worked together, Alex and Rick did not have the same job. Alex used to travel also, but when Nicky was born, he'd requested a transfer to the local group. He now stayed close to home, and even worked from here two days a week.

As lunch progressed, Julianne attempted to make conversation with Rick. He seemed more interested in staring at what there was of her chest than talking. When he did talk, the topic strayed to politics. The more beer he consumed, the more adamant he became about his views of freedom to own guns and the reduction of government intervention and how horrible the president was. Julianne reminded him that he was part of that government machine, but that didn't stop him from spewing. When everyone was finished eating, she jumped up to clear the table, seeking to avoid further confrontation, while Bella wiped little hands.

Julianne brought out the brownies, hugged Bella, and kissed the kids. "I'm beat, gonna call it a day."

"Aw, can't you stay for dessert and horseshoes?"

"No, seriously, I'm dead on my feet."

Rick came over and tried to hug her, but she squirmed free. "Yeah, it was great meeting you. Can I call you?" He again gave her body a visual sweep, this time not even trying to hide it.

"How about if I call you? I can get your number from Alex." She hugged Alex and headed out the door before Edward-Scissor-Hands could try again.

twelve

*J*ulianne stared at the brochure from Father Carmichael. She'd been reading and re-reading it, lost in thought.

"Julianne?"

She startled, surprised to find Dr. Merk standing at the nurses' station. "Oh, sorry, I zoned out for a minute there. What can I do for you Dr. Merk?"

"Please, call me Matt. I'm up here checking on Timothy Jordan. I admitted him from the ER a few hours ago. I saw you and thought I'd say hi. What's that you're reading?"

Julianne handed him the brochure. "It's a brochure my priest gave me about medical missions to Honduras. I'm thinking of using some vacation time to volunteer."

She gazed at him while he read. Matt had a simple, pleasant face. Nothing out of the ordinary, yet there was something comforting about it. Something that felt like home.

He examined the pamphlet. "I might be able to offer some insight if you're looking to do something like this. I've done a couple of trips with Doctors Without Borders."

"Really? That would be great." Julianne glanced at her pendant watch. "I'm heading to the cafeteria for some lunch. Can you take a break?"

He looked at his watch, before checking his cell phone. "Sure, I can break for a while."

"I'm going for some lunch. Can I bring you back anything?" Julianne asked Beverly, one of the other nurses.

"Please." Beverly dug into her pocket and pulled out a ten-dollar bill. "One of those turkey subs and some sour cream and onion chips would be awesome. Thanks!"

Once seated in the cafeteria, Matt said, "One of my stints was in Costa Rico—similar to Honduras in terms of weather and shots. My other stint was in West Africa. I went over to help with Ebola. Man, was that a nightmare. Those hazmat suits are so stifling we could only work about a two-hour shift. I had to be under quarantine when I returned. I'm so glad that outbreak is finally under control." He shook his head. "It killed close to 10,000 people, a huge number of them children."

Julianne had stopped chewing. The idea of going into that sort of environment had never occurred to her. "I don't think I'm cut out to work in an epidemic like that. I'm thinking more of a vaccine clinic or delivery ward."

"Well, in that case, I think the place in this brochure might be just what you're looking for. I would suggest getting your shots as far in advance as possible so they have time to be fully effective."

"Yeah, I think I'll go get them tomorrow so it's all set and I can go whenever. I also need to talk to HR about using vacation or taking a leave."

"They're really good about that here. They encourage us to volunteer overseas. You can go on a short jaunt, say a week or so, to get your feet wet and then decide from there. If you like it, you can always stay longer or return again later."

Matt's phone beeped and vibrated on the table, signaling an end to lunch. "That's me. I need to get back to the ER." He placed his hand on her shoulder and leaned in slightly. "Let me know if you have any more questions, and fill me in when you get back."

She found comfort in the warmth of his hand and realized why she was so at ease with him. *He's like a brother.*

Julianne continued her lunch, contemplating the possibilities in front of her. She knew she could do this. *I mean seriously, what's stopping me? Clay's gone, and I have more vacation than I could ever use. I need to be doing more.*

Part Four

Julianne & Jokob

thirteen

*J*ulianne drove along Forest Park Parkway, her stomach jumbled with butterflies. Although Highway 40 was faster, she preferred the Parkway when she needed extra time to calm her nerves. She arrived early and pulled into the parking lot across from the courthouse. While waiting in her car, she practiced deep breathing, until her phone tweaked with Bella's text tone.

"We're in the parking lot."

"So am I," Julianne texted back. She opened her door and did a visual sweep of the lot. Her poppy and Bella waved. She reached inside her car to grab her purse and briefcase.

Julianne hugged them both. "Thank you for coming. It means a lot for you both to be here." Placing a hand on her poppy's shoulder, she added, "I know how you feel about divorce, Poppy."

"Anything for my *tesoro,*" he replied, giving her a big kiss on each cheek.

They crossed the street together and entered the multi-storied county courthouse building. Although there was a long line of people to go through security, it moved quickly.

Her attorney was waiting on the fourth floor. "We'll stay here until your case is called." She gestured toward some benches outside the courtroom doors.

Her poppy and Bella took seats on either side of Julianne; her attorney stood in front of them. Together, they formed a protective shield around her. Bouncing her legs up and down on the balls of feet, Julianne picked at her fingernails. The inside of her cheek was raw where she'd been chewing it.

"How are you feeling?" her attorney asked, as she flipped through the motion for divorce.

"I'm afraid I might strangle him without you guys. Why couldn't he have agreed to mediation so we could avoid this circus?"

Her poppy laid his hand on hers and said, "You'll do fi—"

"Case #792, Denny vs. Denny." The baritone voice of the court bailiff echoed off the granite walls.

"That's us," her attorney said, rising.

Julianne focused forward to avoid eye contact with Clayton and his attorney coming from the other end of the hallway. But she could still see Clayton glowering at her, his jaw set. Her breath caught.

Bella squeezed one hand, Julianne's attorney the other, and they all entered together. Her poppy and Bella took seats behind Julianne.

Julianne kept her eyes on the judge, deliberately not looking at Clay and his attorney sitting at the next table.

"Denny vs. Denny, Case #792," the judge began. "I've reviewed the documents provided by each party. The only point of contention appears to be an inheritance of $100,000, which the plaintiff is claiming as non-marital property, and the respondent is claiming as marital. I'll start with the respondent. Mr. Denny, please explain why you feel this money should be considered marital property?"

"Your Honor, Nonna, Julianne's grandmother, passed away two years after we married. Nonna was always fond of me and meant for this money to be ours. She mentioned that on several occasions, in front of witnesses." Clay looked straight at the judge, never venturing a glance toward Julianne.

"Ms. Denny?" The judge shifted her attention to Julianne.

"Your Honor, for the 20 years after my grandfather passed away, my nonna… uh, my grandmother, lived with my mom and dad. Much of those twenty years, I also still lived with my parents. Nonna was from the Old Country, and that was simply how it was done. My grandfather was a successful wine merchant and left her in good shape financially. She often spoke of how she wanted any money that remained after she was gone to be divided. Each of her children, grandchildren, and great-grandchildren, if there were any, would receive exactly the same amount regardless of any extenuating circumstances. She felt that was the fairest way to avoid any family feuds."

Julianne looked back at her poppy and Bella, took a deep breath, and continued, "Yes, Nonna was fond of Clayton. She was also devoutly Catholic and felt divorce was a cardinal sin. However, if she were alive today, even she would agree that what Clayton did was grounds for one."

She paused to brush tears away, fighting to regain control over emotions threatening to turn her into a blubbering slob. "Your Honor, Clayton didn't just leave me for another woman. She was pregnant at the time, and didn't even know he was married. I can say unequivocally, that my nonna would not have wanted Clayton to have her money given the circumstances. Also it was left to me in her will, and her son, my father, is here today to attest to her wishes."

She glared at Clayton and snarled, "And *you* do NOT get to call her Nonna."

"Mr. Denny. Do you have any written documentation attesting to your right to these funds?"

"Uh." He shot a look at his attorney, who gave him a quick headshake. "No, Your Honor."

"Well, then it's pretty simple. Given that this money was left to Ms. Denny in her grandmother's will, and barring any documentation to indicate you are entitled to any of it, it is considered non-marital property by the state of Missouri. The respondent's request is denied."

The judge addressed both attorneys, "Is there anything else?"

Clay and his attorney bent their heads together for a brief conference.

"Your Honor, my client feels that in light of this judgment he should at least be entitled to one of their two cats—Ben and Jerry, I believe, are their names."

Julianne's head whipped around and she gave Clay a look she hoped would melt the mid-winter snow and ice covering the street.

"Ms. Denny, what are your feelings regarding this request?"

Julianne stopped glaring at Clay, and shifted her focus to address the judge. "Your Honor, I've had Ben and Jerry since they were three weeks old. A co-worker found them abandoned in an old building and I bottle-raised them. They are now almost four years old. My apartment is the only home they've ever known. Jerry is very timid and would be lost without Ben for support. I don't believe either of them would adapt very well to a change in home."

The judge scribbled some notes on her pad before looking back and forth between parties. "Mr. Denny, I've had cats for decades. Some I've obtained as kittens, some as older rescues. I know how difficult it can be on them to move and upset their routines. Some never recover and can develop destructive behaviors. Separating bonded cats at this age is not in their best interest. Therefore, Mr. Denny, I'm inclined to deny your request for one of the cats and award both of them to Ms. Denny."

"But—" Clay began, but stopped when the judge removed her glasses and raised her eyebrows.

The judge again addressed the attorneys, "Anything else?"

"No, Your Honor," they both answered in unison. The judge rapped her gavel. That quickly it was over—Julianne Denny was once again Julianne Garvoli.

fourteen

Jokob unhitched his red Jeep Wrangler and leveled his thirty-three foot Southwind RV. A few minutes past five and the sun still shone high in the sky, temperatures in the mid-eighties. In the short time it took to complete these tasks, Jokob dripped with sweat. He'd heard St. Louis was humid, but this was ridiculous. He rolled out the awning hoping to deflect some of the heat and set out his zero-gravity lounger. Pulling out his grill, he locked it to the middle axle of the RV. *Steak tonight.*

He stepped into the RV, grabbed a Schlafly's Pale Ale from the fridge, and headed back outside. Settling into the lounger, he popped open the beer and took a long pull. *Hmmm, that is good. The guy at the store was right.*

Jokob dug his phone from his pocket and dialed.

Kevin answered on the second ring. "Hey Joko, buddy. Didya make it to St. Louis?"

"Yup. Sittin' here enjoying a local brew."

"Awesome dude. So how was New Orleans? You go to any titty bars?" Kevin's infectious laugh instantly made people love him.

"Naw, no bars for me, man. But I did have a great visit with the boy. It was good to spend time with him. He's grown so much. Made the varsity team this year. Following in the ole man's footsteps I guess."

"That's great! You're still coming for Zander's birth, right? He's due early September."

"I wouldn't miss it for anything," Jokob replied, suppressing the lump in his throat. He didn't want his dark memories to usurp his friend's joyous occasion. He quickly changed the subject. "I've been following your weight-loss journey on Facebook. What is it, a hundred pounds for far? Proud of you man."

"One-twenty and counting. Nothing like a heart scare to push me into gear, eh? I didn't want my son to lose his dad before he could even be born. I already feel so much better. Sixty left to go. And Ammuri's been able to maintain a healthy pregnancy weight since she cooks such satisfying food for me."

"She's been a positive influence on you, that's for sure. So how goes the game testing business?" Jokob asked, realizing he hadn't in a while.

"It's hit or miss, feast or famine. So, pretty much the way it's always been. But we get by. It helps that Ammuri makes good money."

"Glad to hear it."

"So what's your plan there in St. Louis?"

"My show opens in two days. Ya know, I've been on the road non-stop for three years straight. I think I might be getting tired of this routine. The shows pay the bills, but the hype and pomp is wearing thin. I wish I could take pictures and leave the rest of it to someone else. I know it sounds weird to say I need a change, when I spend my time traveling around the country, but I'm feeling like it doesn't fit me anymore."

"Have you considered settling down, or staying somewhere longer than three months? You're always welcome to hang out in the Seattle area for as long as you want."

Jokob heard the tension in Kevin's voice—treading carefully with the subject after their big blow-up two years earlier when he'd suggested Jokob come live in Seattle.

"I've thought about it, but what would I do? I had an offer to curate the gallery in New Orleans, but I can't see myself doing the same thing every day." Jokob headed back into the RV for another beer. He put the phone on speaker while he added tenderizer to the steaks he'd had thawing in the fridge since leaving New Orleans two days earlier.

Jokob settled back into his lounger and sighed heavily. "I still miss her."

"I know buddy. It's gonna take some time."

"There's a huge hole in me and I don't see how time's gonna fill that." Jokob became quiet and stared at the orange and pink beginnings of a sunset. He always tried to position his RV so he could see the sunset each evening. It was something he had shared with her.

"Hey, I need to get supper cooking. Good talkin' to you man."

"You too. And don't forget—September tenth."

fifteen

I don't want to." Julianne had her phone on speaker and placed tiny red, pink, and purple petunias into her deck planters.

"Come on, Jules. It'll be fun," Bella pleaded. "You haven't gone anywhere 'cept work in months. Before the exhibit, we could have dinner at that cute little outdoor café that recently opened a couple of blocks from you."

Julianne snorted and replied, "Why would I want to go to some artsy fartsy photo exhibit by some guy who's probably gay and thinks he's God's gift to film? Once I'm done with my flowers, there's a quart of *Blue Bunny Rocky Road* with my name on it, and a new Nicholas Sparks novel. I'm set. And besides, I have too been out—remember those three god-awful blind dates you forced me to go on?"

"Jules… I'll meet you there at 5." Bella hung up.

Bella had spoken, and Julianne knew it would do no good to argue. The only way to silence her was to go. She could have peace for a few more months before she'd have to play it out again. She didn't want to date, yet Bella kept setting her up. She had her work and a mission trip to plan. The last thing she needed was some man to come along and mess things up.

Julianne selected tan strappy sandals and an above-the-knee-length sundress covered in bright yellow sunflowers, one she hadn't worn since two summers ago. She loved the way it swished against her knees, as she sashayed toward the café, and even found herself smiling. She had to admit it felt good to get dressed up and go out for a change. In the fourteen months since Clay left, Julianne had set up a safe, if somewhat boring, routine: work, pick up food at Marco's, and home to a book or movie. Those three horrible dates Bella had arranged had been enough to convince her that all men were either scum or helpless and needed mommies, and she wasn't up for any of it. But she had been growing restless lately and couldn't figure out why.

She arrived at Bon Aire just late enough to convince Bella she wasn't coming.

They both ordered the house Merlot—wine happy hour so they each got two—and they made small talk while awaiting their meal. Julianne knew something was up; they never made small talk.

"OK, so what gives?" Julianne raised her eyebrows at her friend.

"Nothing. What do you mean?"

"You're acting weird."

"Okay look, there's this really cute single guy at work, and—"

Julianne cut her off. "Stop doing this. I've told you. I. Am. Not. Interested." She emphasized each word with a rap of her nails on the table edge.

"Jules, it's been over a year. You can't quit living because of one jerky guy."

"'That jerky guy,' as you call him, was my husband. He cheated on me, or did you forget? Left me without even the decency of an honest goodbye. Oh and what about the three guys I have been out with, you know, the ones you thought would be perfect for me? And let's not forget that grabby guy Alex invited to the BBQ last summer. But you're right, I can't let one jerky guy ruin my life. I should date them all and spread the ruination around."

"Don't be mean. I'm only trying to help."

"Stop. I'm fine."

Bella held up her hands in surrender. "Okay, okay, I get it. I just want you to be happy."

"I am happy. I don't need a man to be happy, although there are times…" Julianne winked at Bella, and they both roared laughing.

The waiter brought their check, and as he moved away, Bella whispered a bit too loudly, "He's kinda cute. Nice ass."

Julianne tossed her napkin at her. "Eeerrr"

They paid their checks and strolled the two blocks to the gallery.

Julianne stared, mesmerized by the photo, surprised by the feelings rumbling up from within. *I've never seen anything so totally sad.* She wondered what the artist had in mind when he shot this one. In spite of herself, she found herself enjoying the exhibit. The photos seemed to speak to her.

"What do you see?"

A deep, slightly husky voice, with no discernible accent, startled her. She'd been so intent on the picture she hadn't noticed there was someone standing barely more than a breath away.

"It's so sad," she replied, without looking at the speaker. She continued to stare, pulled into the scene, as if to become a part of it.

"Tell me more."

"I can't. It's inside me. It... It makes me want to cry. I feel such loss and regret."

"I've probably asked a hundred people that question over the past three months and you're the only one who's seen that."

Julianne opened her eyes, startled to recognize the ruggedly handsome face as that of the photographer. She blushed, embarrassed at her description. "I'm sorry. I didn't mean to—"

"No, that's not it. I meant that you're the only one who gets it. That sees beyond the obvious and feels it. You have a rare gift. Thank you."

Julianne blushed even deeper, as he offered his hand. "Jokob O'Callaghan."

"Julianne Garvoli, but most people call me Jules."

He grinned and she melted, allowing herself the briefest glimpse into his intense crystal-green eyes.

"You go to many exhibits?"

"My first actually," not mentioning that Bella practically had to drag her there.

"Close your eyes."

"What?"

"I want you to try something. Close your eyes."

Julianne did as requested and waited, thinking this odd but inexplicably wanting to please this intriguing stranger.

"What do you see?"

"Nothing silly, my eyes are closed," with a silent *DUH* to herself, much less inhibited after those two glasses of Merlot.

"Feel what you saw earlier, and tell me what you see in the top left corner." Jokob cupped his hand under her right elbow and leaned in close.

She took a deep breath and her mind's eye found details she hadn't consciously realized were there. "There's a clock tower. The time is 2:25."

"And now the lower right corner."

"There's an old man, sitting on a park bench, petting a scruffy white dog. He's leaning on a wooden cane."

"Middle?" Jokob continued to guide her through the photo.

"Kids in a cross walk, walking away, past the old man." A lump rose in her throat. "That's it. That's what looks so sad. He's looking at them with longing, like there's someone..." Julianne fluttered her eyes open. "Missing." She couldn't stop herself from staring into the deepest sparkling green eyes she'd ever seen.

Jokob nodded in agreement, not taking his gaze off her. "I shot it about ten years ago in a Polish neighborhood in New York. I was there researching my maternal roots. This whole wall is from that series," he said, gesturing to other photos in a similar sepia style.

"I was staying on this street with my aunt and noticed this old man at the cross walk every day, so I started shooting. I must've shot three rolls before I got one that captured it."

"Rolls?"

He chuckled. "I'm old fashioned, I prefer to work with film. It forces me to take my time and really get into the mood of the shot."

"Did you ever talk to him?"

"On my last day there," Jokob said, nodding. "I brought him a cup of coffee and we chatted on that bench. His name was Leopold and he had come over from Poland as a young man. He lost his only son early in the Vietnam War. Three weeks later, his daughter-in-law died in a tragic accident. She was eight months pregnant. The baby, his only grandson, also died."

"How horrible," she said, the same rush of sadness flooding her senses.

"He had always dreamed of waiting for his grandchildren at that very cross walk. So now he goes there every day and watches the children. He said it feeds his soul." Jokob paused and again looked into Julianne's eyes. "I find that photography heals mine."

Jokob placed his hand on the small of Julianne's back and guided her past several photos, explaining some as he went.

The heat of his hand on her back sent tingles up her spine, and Julianne felt lighter than she had in months as they wandered, talking and laughing.

At the end of that wall, Jokob stopped and looked around. "Julianne, my apologies, but I must get back to mingling. I am the artist after all." He shrugged and laughed.

His laughter was music to her ears. Jokob's fingers brushed lightly against hers, as he handed Julianne his card, and she caught her breath.

"I'd like to do more of this." Jokob said. "Would you have dinner with me?"

"Jokob, you're really nice, and you take great pictures, but," she shook her head, "I don't date."

He shrugged. "Neither do I. But I do eat," he replied with that same beguiling grin, deep dimples peeking out from his reddish beard.

She couldn't help but move closer, catching a wisp of his unique musk.

"Uh, I don't know." She tilted her head slightly and stared into those eyes that seemed to spark with crystal facets. *Am I flirting?* She stifled a giggle.

"Perhaps come on a photo shoot with me. With your knack for detail, you might enjoy it, and I'd welcome the company. I'll be in the area for three months before I head off to Seattle for my next assignment," he said over his shoulder, walking away.

She shook her head, realizing she'd been staring at his toned backside. *Geez… what am I doing?* Unable to stop herself, she leaned a bit to the right and continued to watch.

Julianne stepped to the edge of life for a quick peek, torn between competing selves, one inexplicably wanting to spend as much time as possible with this stranger, the other convinced most men were scum.

After Jokob joined a couple at a photo across the room, Bella ran up giggling, grabbing Julianne by the arm. "Oh my gawd! Jeez was that the artist? Hunka, hunka. What'd he give you?"

"His card. I might buy a picture," she replied, tucking a freshly cut curl behind her ear and doing her best to disguise the grin welling up from inside. His invitation would remain her little secret for now.

sixteen

On a stool at her kitchen island, Julianne flipped the card over and over between her fingers, deep in thought. She dialed and hung up several times. *I don't want to go on a date.* She reminded herself what he'd said.

What could it hurt? She dialed, hoping he wouldn't answer, but pleasantly surprised when he did.

"Um, hi? This is Julianne Garvoli? We met at your exhibit last week?" She hadn't felt this nervous since the time in sixth grade when she'd called a boy she had a crush on. *What was his name again? Oh yeah, Tony something-or-other.*

"Of course, I remember," he jumped in. "I was hoping you'd call. Look, I'm planning an outing in Alton tomorrow. They're predicting gorgeous weather. Come with me."

It wasn't a question, more like a challenge and before she could stop herself by over-thinking it, she agreed, "Sure. When?"

"I'll pick you up at four."

"P.M., right?" *Please god let it not be A.M..*

"Nope, sorry. I want to get some sunrise shots of the bridge."

"Ugh. You do realize that normal people don't get up before the crack of dawn?" Although a morning person for sure, this was early even for her.

Jokob let loose a laugh that tingled from the top of her head to her toes. "Yeah, I've been told I'm not quite normal."

Julianne gave him her address, still surprised at her newfound boldness. "OK. I'll see you at four. I'll come down so you can wait outside."

"Wait," Jokob said hastily, "You probably already know this but, dress in layers. It's liable to be a bit chilly on the river that early, even in June. See ya."

Julianne hung up and said to the walls, "Holy shit! Now what am I getting myself into?"

Julianne emerged from her building stifling a yawn, still not sure this whole thing was such a good idea. *What in blue blazes am I thinking, getting up before dawn to go lord knows where, with a man I don't know?* One look at the grinning, bearded stranger, leaning casually against his red Jeep Wrangler, reminded her why. *He sure is easy on the eyes.* Jokob held open the door and she climbed in. She surprised herself by allowing her gaze to follow his movements to the other side of the Jeep.

"Feel free to adjust the station to whatever you want." Jokob gestured to the radio buttons.

"Actually this is one of my favorites," Julianne said, as the comforting strains of a Miranda Lambert song wafted from the stereo. Unlike most of her friends who wouldn't be caught dead listening to country, she loved it, especially the more modern groups, like Lady Antebellum and Mumford and Sons.

"So are you native to St. Louis?" Jokob asked between GPS interruptions.

"Yes, I grew up in a neighborhood called The Hill. Mostly Italian-American families. But if you're gonna be here for three months, you must learn the right question to ask. Around here it's 'What high school did you go to?'"

"What high school?" he asked.

"Yes. In truth, though no one ever admits it, it's a way of determining where someone might be on the socioeconomic scale. I attended Rosati-Kain, the girl's Catholic High School. With my olive skin tone and facial features I got from my Italian dad, and my light hair and eyes from my Irish momma—let's just say it confused the heck out of everyone." Julianne allowed a little giggle to slip out as she became more comfortable around Jokob.

"How 'bout you? Where'd you grow up?" Julianne asked, trying not to stare at him.

"Everywhere. I was an Army brat so I literally grew up everywhere. My dad retired right before I started high school, and we finally settled in Cape Cod. Dad took up fishing, with his sights on local politics. It was nice to belong somewhere during high school, but I was still the new kid, at least until I proved myself on the football field. I made the varsity team my sophomore year. I was the star tight-end, destined for college scholarships until a 250 pound tackle took me out in the third game of my junior year. Spiral break of my left tibia. Never healed properly, and my dream of an NFL career was over before it ever had a chance."

"Look at me, monopolizing the conversation." Jokob laughed and grinned at Julianne, flashing those dimples.

"It's fine. I'm enjoying hearing about your life."

"Well, if you're sure?" Jokob shrugged. "That's when I found photography, or rather, it found me. Oh, not right away… first, I had to throw myself a huge pity party—you know how seventeen-year-old boys can be."

"I thought that was just girls."

"Naw, it's guys, too. So, one day Coach handed me a camera and said, 'Here kid, make yourself useful.'" Jokob did his best Cape Cod accent, which got them both laughing.

They approached the Clark Bridge heading into Alton. Still dark, the lights danced on the Mississippi River.

"Amazing," Jokob said, slowing and pointing at the water. "That goes on my list. But, not today. Today will be perfect for something else."

He steered left off the bridge, and immediately left again into the park by the amphitheater. "I drove out here yesterday to scout for locations." He pulled in and parked as close as possible to his chosen spot. He hopped out and unloaded camera gear.

"There's coffee in the thermos, tea and breakfast bagel sandwiches in the ice chest. Help yourself whenever you'd like. And that," he said, pointing to a concrete building about 100 yards away, "is the restroom. We should have the place to ourselves for a while. I've been told few people get up this early."

Julianne swore he winked at her. She watched as Jokob hoisted the shoulder bag, picked up the tripods, and headed toward the fence.

"Can I help with anything?" she asked, feeling a little less than useless.

"Ha! Can you tell I'm used to working alone?" Jokob laughed and handed her the two smaller tripods.

They walked out to the end of a fenced area, as far as they possibly could to get the best angle for the sunrise.

"Wow. That's one huge camera," Julianne remarked, as Jokob stabilized the large tripod and sighted in the biggest camera she'd ever seen.

Jokob reached into his bag and pulled out a smaller one. "Here, I brought this for you," he said, holding it out to her.

"Me?" Julianne said, backing away, her hands up, palms facing toward him. "Um, I'm not good at taking pictures, actually more like I suck at it."

"Nonsense. Anyone can take pictures. Granted, it takes time and patience to become really good, and most people can't turn it into art, but decent pictures are simply a matter of doing a few basic things right. Besides, it's digital, so if you truly suck at it, we delete everything and it's our little secret."

His easy manner helped Julianne feel a bit less insecure. She took the camera and slung it over her shoulder. "What should I take pictures of?"

"Anything that captures your attention. When you see something that interests you, aim, take a breath, let it out, and press this button." He leaned in as he showed her, his hand brushing against hers.

Julianne felt the same rush of excitement she'd felt at the gallery. *Oh my.*

It wasn't quite sunrise. Even though the light was limited, Julianne looked through the viewfinder anyway and started scanning. She hovered for a while, focusing on Jokob as he completed his setup. She even snapped a few pictures, fascinated by his patience.

As the sun climbed, Jokob began shooting, moving between the three cameras with ease and skill. Julianne gawked in awe. She alternated between taking shots of him and her own version of the sunrise. She forced herself to take, but not look at any of the pictures. If there was a bad one, she would stop, but she was actually having fun.

About an hour after they'd arrived, the sun was high on the horizon, and the photo shoot was over. After packing the cameras and tripods safely away in a lockbox in the back of the Jeep, they decided on breakfast at one of the picnic tables. Jokob had insisted she hang onto the camera he'd loaned her, and while they ate, he scanned the pictures on the display.

"It's been a while since anyone took pictures of me working."

Julianne noted sadness in his voice, but decided now wasn't the best time to ask questions.

"You've got some decent sunrise shots in here. Very interesting angles."

"You're just saying that." Julianne blushed, but found she enjoyed his praise. *Strange, I don't recall Clayton ever telling me I was good at anything.*

"Hey," he said, changing the subject. "I was thinking of doing some exploring up the Great River Road. Are you up for some more adventure, or have I bored you to death already?"

"I'd love to. It's been ages since I was out this way. That is, if you don't mind me taking more pictures of

116

you working." *Damn girl... you are flirting with him. What are you thinking?*

They loaded the ice chest into the Jeep and took off west toward Grafton. Jokob spotted a turnout next to the cliffs overlooking the Mississippi River and pulled over. They got out of the Jeep and crunched across the gravel parking lot to the cliff wall.

As they stared up at the yellow and red dragon-like Piasa Bird with massive teeth emerging from red lips, Julianne explained, "No one knows how it came to be painted on the cliff wall. The creature was given its name by the Illini Indians in the 1600's, 'The Piasa,' meaning a bird that devours men."

"I'd heard it was big, but this is magnificent. How do we get up there?" he asked, gesturing overhead.

"We don't. Well, actually it's possible, but it's blocked off because of teens going up there to party and getting hurt."

"Too bad, I love exploring." He used one of his medium cameras, moving around the bird, taking pictures from various angles, including Julianne in some of them.

"Shall we keep going?" he asked, heading back toward the Jeep.

Julianne simply grinned in response. She was thoroughly enjoying herself and hadn't had this much fun in a long time. If she was honest with herself, she'd stopped having fun way before Clay left.

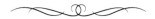

A few miles before they reached the city limits sign for Grafton, Jokob pulled off the road and let the Jeep idle. Julianne looked at him and followed his line of sight to a billboard with a picture of a man, mouth wide open, dangling from a wire. The caption read Grafton Zipline.

"Are you game?" Jokob looked over at Julianne and winked.

She had only heard about the crazy sounding experience that involved high-strung wire, some kind of harness, and throwing yourself off into space.

"Ziplining?" Julianne's voice bumped up a few octaves. "You're kidding, right? I don't know about me playing Jane to your Tarzan." Her nails dug into the door handle, her face as white as the few fluffy clouds drifting overhead.

"Come on, it's completely safe. I've done it all over the country. Any place that has one, I'm on it. I've even started a new photo exhibit and book called *Flight*. It features some of the amazing views only available to those who venture out onto the wire. I promise you'll love it."

"How 'bout you go and I'll watch and cheer you on."

"Well, you can't really do that. Once you're on the course, there's no way to the next stand except via the line."

Julianne raised her eyebrows and chewed her lower lip. Her insides trembled. *Where's my sense of adventure?*

Continuing along the Great River Road into Grafton, Jokob hung a right and headed up a steep, gravel-topped hill. He patted her arm as he turned into the parking lot. "I guarantee you'll love it, and if you don't, you can stop."

"Uh." Julianne remained steadfastly in the Jeep, seat belt firmly fastened. Jokob came around to her side, leaned across, and unclipped her seatbelt, grinning the whole time. He took her hand and led her up to the check-in office.

"Two please," Jokob told the tank-top-wearing-muscle-builder guy at the check-in. "One experienced and," he said, jerking her thumb in Julianne's direction, "one terrified newbie."

"Hi, I'm Terry. I'll be your guide for the next tour, along with Suzette and Billy." Looking at Julianne, he winked and said, "Don't worry, we get that a lot. We actually have a beginner line, sort of like the bunny slope in skiing, but way safer." He pointed to a group of six people already geared and waiting. "We were just fixin' to get going."

Terry dug through a green plastic bin for harnesses that would fit each of them. Motioning to Julianne, he said, "Come over here, little lady, and I'll get you fitted for your gear."

"Gear?" Julianne gulped but stepped closer.

He laid her harness on the floor and pointed at the two circles formed by the straps. "OK. Put a foot into each of these two openings."

Julianne did as instructed.

Terry raised the harness up her legs until it reached the top. "Here, hold this for a second." He stepped around her and brought the straps up and over her shoulders, hooking each with heavy-duty carabiners. He circled to the front and pulled on the ends until they formed a tightly fitted harness.

His easy manner relaxed Julianne a bit, and as he performed the same procedure for Jokob, she watched.

Terry called everyone together, checked their gear, and outlined the safety instructions.

"First, never ever, ever and I mean NEVER, touch the wire. You WILL lose a finger, if not worse. Second, during the zip, don't put your hands on the top of the gears over your head. Again, you WILL lose a finger and there's a good chance your entire hand will get trapped and ripped to shreds. And none of us wants to hang onto the ramp while a helicopter hovers and attempts to rescue you."

Julianne tentatively held up her hand. "I thought this was supposed to be safe."

Terry laughed. "It is, little lady, unless you're a moron and don't follow those two rules I've explained. Beyond that, there are only two more rules. Third, when it's your turn, I will connect your harness to the wire. Do NOT go until Billy gives thumbs up from the other side. Fourth, when you reach the end, try not to kick Billy in the balls when he helps you stop. He really doesn't like that, and it can delay us moving on to the next ramp. Any questions?"

Boisterous laugher prevented questions.

"Okay, we got four newbie's on this tour so we're going to start with the beginner line. But honestly, we'd start there anyway since it's, well, the first line, and we kinda hafta start there. After that, if any of you changes her mind," he said, winking at Julianne, "and wants off the tour, Suzette will escort you back here to wait. But trust me, after that first zip, you won't want to stop. Ever."

They hiked the quarter mile to the first line—short with an easy entrance and exit. "Me first," squealed Dee Dee, the youngest in the group.

Julianne felt a little silly being so scared. *If an eight-year-old can do it, so can I.*

Billy's job was to assist the riders, when they reached the landing zone, so he hooked up his harness and zipped on over. He would also rescue anyone who became stuck in the middle.

Terry hooked Dee Dee's harness to the wire, and as soon as Billy gave the thumbs up, she jumped off the platform with absolutely no hesitation, screaming with delight. The friction of the gear over the wire whirred, and the sound echoed off the bluffs. Once she reached the landing platform, she spun around, did a victory punch and yelled back to her dad, "Woo Hoo! Again!"

"That's my girl!"

Julianne's mouth dried, as if she'd eaten cotton. She bit her lower lip, knees knocking together. Knowing her anxiety would simply get worse the longer she waited, she stepped forward. "I'll go," she said, her voice hitching.

Terry hooked her up and reminded her to never touch the line itself. She inched up to the edge of the platform and peered over the edge. The ground wasn't far down but still the idea of her throwing herself out into thin air chilled her to her core. She took a deep breath, yelled "Geronomo!" and sort of half-sat, half-stepped off the edge, holding on to the bar for dear life. She was grinning from ear-to-ear and laughing by the time her feet touched down. Shooting Jokob a thumbs up, she knew she, too, was hooked for life.

When Jokob hit the exit ramp, she jumped up and down in front of him, like an excited six-year-old. He laughed. "Another convert I see."

They continued on the tour, each ride longer and more complex than the last, until they reached the last line—2000 feet with a steep drop that leveled out near the end.

Terry stepped in front of the group. "On this one, if you're too light, you might stop in the middle. If that happens, no worries. Billy has a pulley system he'll use to drag you to the ramp. So if that happens, simply enjoy the view. Dee Dee, I'm afraid you'll have to ride tandem with Billy on this one—you're guaranteed to stick since you're so tiny."

"Tiny, but mighty!" Dee Dee whooped, and jumped up to ride over with Billy.

Jokob took the small camera Julianne had used before and put the strap around her neck. "If you get stuck, enjoy the view and take lots of pictures. I'm going first on this one so I can get some shots of everyone coming across."

Terry hooked him up. Jokob adjusted his action video camera to his head and took a running start, leaping off the landing. He had no issue getting across.

When Julianne got up for her turn, it suddenly dawned on her that she might get stuck. Raising her eyebrows, she stepped up to the edge and looked down. *It's a really long way down.*

Once Terry had her connected, she didn't hesitate. She ran to the edge of the platform and leaped into open air. As she approached the low spot, she slowed. *No, no, please no.*

"No, no, come on," she yelled. She continued to slow and stopped completely a little more than half way across. She tried bouncing up and down and wiggling side-to-side. Nothing doing. She was stuck. *Oh well.* She took out the camera and, with trepidation, released the handle and began shooting. She realized how peaceful and beautiful it was hanging out up here and wished Billy would take his time.

Billy gave her a few minutes before he began pulling her toward the ramp with the lever system. After she completed her slow decent, Jokob came up and gave her a high five. "I was afraid that might happen. What are you, about a hundred pounds soaking wet?" He winked, picked her up under her arms, and let her hang like dead weight.

"A hundred five, actually." She tried to sound surly but was laughing too hard to pull it off.

When the tour reached its end, Julianne yelled, "More! Let's go again!" She'd had an awesome time and would definitely be doing this again.

"Do you like wine?"

"You have no idea," Julianne giggled. "Absolutely—red, white, blush, pretty much anything but Chardonnay. You might say it's in my blood."

"There's a winery and restaurant up the road. You hungry?"

"Starving."

"Good, me too."

Their timing was perfect, and with no crowd, they placed their orders almost at once. While waiting, they tasted wines. Finding something each liked, they purchased glasses, and found a secluded table by the window overlooking the river.

"So, how'd you like your first photo shoot?" Jokob asked.

"It was fun. But do they all start before the crack of dawn?"

"I only did that for your benefit."

Julianne's brows shot up, her eyes forming a wide circle. Her jaw dropped.

Seeing her reaction, he laughed. "I'm teasing." He sipped some wine and asked, "So, what's your story?"

"My… story?" she replied, a flush bloomed on her neck.

"Yeah, I see glimpses of it when you think I'm not looking. You seem like you're really far way. You've obviously been through a lot with something. Or someone."

Not sure why she felt so comfortable with this handsome stranger, Julianne looked into his eyes again, mesmerized by the twinkling green, and quickly away. She took a deep breath before beginning.

"I never pictured myself married, let alone divorced by twenty-six. I pictured myself traveling, helping others, and doing adventurous things. I had these dreams of spending part of each year in Central and South America, perhaps Guatemala, Costa Rico, Peru, Argentina… somewhere like that, volunteering in the hospitals or orphanages. I even took six years of Spanish in school, and went on two mission trips with my church youth group during high school. It's the primary reason I became a nurse. Meeting Clay changed everything."

"Husband?"

Julianne grimaced, biting her lower lip. She nodded. "Clayton and I met my second year of nursing at St. Louis University. He was in his final year of the Pharmacy Tech Program. He'd considered going all the way and becoming a Pharmacist, but backed out. There was something magical about him. I don't know how he did it, but somehow he made me forget myself, my dreams.

We were inseparable from the start and got married during my senior year, after he'd graduated. The idea of his new wife traveling to some bug-infested jungle was ludicrous to him and he would hear nothing of it. He wanted me to eventually stay home and raise babies. I guess I convinced myself I wanted that too." She paused and sipped more wine. "Don't get me wrong, I love my work as a nurse. It's just…," she frowned and said, "I wanted other things too, and didn't realize until after he left how much of myself I'd given up to be with him. I wasn't always so afraid to try new things."

"Kind of old fashioned, eh?" Jokob said with a sideways grin and tilted eyebrow.

"So much for old fashioned. I came home a little over a year ago and he was gone. Left me for a Pharmaceutical rep with big boobs and bleached blonde hair. Not even a real, decent goodbye either. He left a note on a greasy In-Out Taco receipt." A blush ran from her chest to her face. She stared down at her food. The whole divorce mess still embarrassed and shamed her.

Hearing Jokob laughing hysterically, the color deepened in her cheeks. "I'm sorry. You find the fact that my husband left me for another woman funny?" she said, unable to keep the sarcasm from her voice.

"Hilarious! Not that your husband left you like that, that's despicable. But don't you see the humor in your husband leaving you for a traveling saleswoman? It's a reversal of the classic cliché." Jokob laughed so hard he could barely choke out this explanation.

Julianne quirked her lips and rapped her nails on the table. Slowly a grin peeked out from behind her wrinkled brow. Watching Jokob bent over at the waist, practically rolling-on-the-floor-laughing, she lost the battle when a single giggle escaped, followed by another, erupting into full-fledged-tears-rolling-down-her-cheeks laughter. She didn't know if she was laughing or crying, but she didn't stop until her belly ached.

"You know, in the past year, not one of my friends has had the guts to point that out to me. Thank you." She dabbed under her eyes, sure her mascara had rac-cooned her by now, but she didn't care. This felt good, better in fact than she'd ever felt.

After lunch, Jokob pulled a smaller camera bag out of the Jeep. They strolled across the street and down to the river.

"It's so beautiful here." Jokob placed the case on a rock and faced the river. "I'm always amazed at the sheer power of a river in spring." He knelt and flipped open the lid.

Julianne spied a photo of a stunning, beautiful red-head slipped into the top cover. It was impossible to miss, so she asked, "Who's that?" *I hope it's a sister*.

"That's Keara." Jokob let the breath escape his lips heavily, and grazed a finger gently across the photo-graph. "My wife."

Julianne swallowed hard, trying to hide her dismay, her guts alternating between shock and disappointment. *Well, he did tell me he didn't date*. "You're married?" she managed to squeak out, barely above a whisper.

Jokob looked out at the river. "I was." His voice cracked. "She died. Breast cancer. Three years ago."

126

Julianne gasped. "I'm so sorry. She was… beautiful."

Jokob closed the case and stood up, hoisting the bag back onto his shoulder. "Yes, she was." He began walking slowly toward the Jeep. "Do you mind if we call it a day? I've got tons of work to do before my next outing."

"Of course." Julianne wanted to ask if she'd said something wrong but held back.

As the Jeep pulled up to her apartment, Julianne found herself wishing the day wasn't over. It was still early, not even five o'clock. She liked this guy and she'd had fun. But something had shifted with Jokob since the river. He'd been quiet on the drive back, almost moody. *I shouldn't have asked about that picture.* She mentally knocked herself upside the head. "You wanna come up?"

Jokob turned off the Jeep, sitting silently for a few minutes. Julianne fidgeted with the door handle. Finally, he opened his door and slowly made his way around to her side. He opened Julianne's door, held out his hand, and helped her out.

"I… " He shook his head, looking at his feet. "I can't. I have work to do tonight and another early day tomorrow. It was fun having you along today. If you'd like to go out in the field again while I'm here, I'd welcome your company."

He looked up and the sparkle was gone, replaced by something empty and hollow. He sighed, walked around, and climbed into the driver's seat.

"I'd like that. Call me," Julianne said through the open top of the Jeep. She watched him drive away before heading to her apartment. She had the next two days off and only hoped she could sleep after this day.

As soon as she got inside, she texted Bella. "Lunch at 1 tomorrow-Café Ventana?"

She waited for Bella's reply—"YES!!!" and headed to the kitchen for a glass of wine. She settled in front of her laptop and zoned out reading email and Facebook, thinking about her day.

seventeen

I spent all day yesterday with that photographer," Julianne said, practically bouncing in her seat, barely able to control her enthusiasm, as they waited for menus.

Bella's eyes grew wide as saucers. "What? Spill it! I want every detail, every tiny morsel."

"Well it wasn't a date or anything. He took me on a photo shoot at the Alton Bridge." Julianne felt like her smile might break her face. "We explored the bluffs at the Piasa Bird, zip-lined, had lunch at The Grafton Winery and—"

Bella interrupted her. "You what lined?"

"Zip-lining, I'm sure you've heard of it."

"I have, but I can't imagine you doing it."

"And just why not?"

"Uh, little miss doesn't like wind in her face, is why not."

"Well I did it and had a blast. You and Alex should go sometime."

"Ok, so spill it. Tell me about this guy."

"Bella, I had so much fun. I really like him, he's sweet and funny and as you saw at his show, gorgeous and talented. And oh my, he's got the deepest crystal-green eyes with streaks of gold. I've never seen eyes quite that color."

"Are you sure they aren't contacts?" Bella winked.

"I suppose they could be… but don't ruin my fantasy." Julianne laughed. She loved how Bella could always make her laugh.

"There's only one problem. I'm not sure if he likes me that way. Or even if he can like me. He's got some big issues."

"Yeah, so who doesn't?"

"No, I mean soul damaging issues. His wife died three years ago."

"Ugh. Yeah, that's an issue. Well it's been three years, so maybe…" Bella shrugged hopefully.

The waitress interrupted them, and they both ordered their usual Caesar salads and iced tea.

"He told me at the show that he doesn't date. I told him the same thing. What do I do? I've been out of the dating game so long I don't even know how it's played anymore. Not that I ever really knew considering how little I dated before I met Clay. I didn't think I'd let myself fall for anyone, or be able to after what Clay did to me, but this guy's got me thinking that maybe, just maybe, not all men are scum." Julianne pushed her salad from one side of the plate to the other and stabbed at a tomato, too excited to eat much.

"Are there plans to meet again?"

"Nothing specific." Julianne sipped her tea. "But he did say he'd welcome my company out in the field again." Julianne echoed the words Jokob had said while she chewed on a fingernail instead of eating.

"He'd welcome your company in the field?" Bella emphasized each word. "Not very romantic."

"I said it wasn't a date. I have his number but don't want to seem pushy, or worse, overly anxious and needy. Heck, he might run."

"Hey, don't sell yourself short. Give him a few days, and if he doesn't call, you should call him."

"Or if he doesn't call me, maybe he's just not ready. Or worse, not into me. Geez, what am I, twelve?" Julianne grimaced.

Bella laughed her outrageously infectious laugh. "I'm so glad I'm not still out there. Come to think of it, I've never been 'out there,'" she emphasized with air quotes. "I'd much rather be chasing my rug rats than chasing men."

Julianne raised an eyebrow. "Well, it's not like I had much choice in that matter. Besides this guy's got possibilities."

Bella glanced at her watch, jumped up, took out a ten and a five, and laid them on the table. "Well girlie, I gotta run and relieve the sitter while my house is still standing." She hugged Julianne. "Call me if anything happens. Don't you dare leave me hanging."

The phone was ringing when Julianne unlocked her door after her morning run. She sprinted across her apartment, dodging cats as she raced to get there in time. The caller-id showed unknown, which she usually didn't answer, but this time she did, hoping.

"Hello?" she answered, breathless.

"Hi Julianne, it's Jokob. The photographer? I'm sorry I haven't called sooner, but I was working and then, can you believe it, I didn't have your number. My cell phone crashed, and I lost all my caller-id info. Lucky for me, your landline is a listed number."

Thank you, Poppy. For once Julianne was glad her poppy had insisted she keep a landline no matter how archaic it seemed. She was delighted Jokob had made the effort.

131

"Oh that's okay, I've been working too," she replied, though after a week she had been wondering if he'd ever call.

"Um," Jokob hesitated. "Look, I'm not real sure how to ask this, so I'll just throw it out there. I know I told you that I don't date, and I don't, or at least I haven't. And I know you told me you don't either. To be honest, I don't know if I'm ready, but I think I'd like to try. I'd like to ask you out, not to a photo shoot, but on an actual date. Would you consider having dinner with me?"

Julianne could tell this was difficult for him. "Yes," she said, doing a little happy dance. She hadn't realized how much she wanted him to ask. "Where?"

"You pick, since you're from around here."

"Okay. Do you like Italian?"

"Mi piace la cucina italina."

"I'm impressed." Julianne giggled at Jokob's attempt to say "I like Italian cooking" in Italian.

"I pick up a lot of stray info living on the road."

"Great, pick me up at six and I'll introduce you to The Hill. The atmosphere is sort of dressy casual."

Julianne raced through a shower and rummaged through the closet, selecting and discarding half a dozen outfits. She finally settled on a sweet, blue scooped-neck blouse that showed off her petite figure. One of the few she owned that required a bra, but for this occasion, she decided she'd suffer. Combined with black, skintight leggings and ankle boots, she thought she looked pretty damned hot. She felt great, too, excited to be going on a date with someone she'd picked, and liked, instead of a blind date. As she finished her makeup, the doorbell rang. "Hang on," she called out, as she ran for the door. *He's early.*

She peeked through the peephole before cracking the door ajar. "What the hell are you doing here?"

Clay whistled. "Wow. You look nice." He gave her the once over and whistled again approvingly.

"That's a little inappropriate don't you think?" Julianne propped her right foot against the bottom of the door, leaving it open about shoulder width but blocking his entrance. She had her right hand on the door, her left fist on her hip.

"You need to leave, I have plans. Why are you here anyway?"

"I was in the neighborhood and wanted to see Ben and Jerry."

"That's ridiculous, you can't just drop by. We're divorced. Besides, you've shown no interest in seeing them in the past six months, so why now?"

"Actually, it's my birthday and I missed you." Clayton's words slurred a bit getting this out.

Julianne caught a whiff of alcohol on his breath and put her hand up to her face. "You're drunk. But Happy Birthday," she said, not wanting to be completely heartless.

A throat cleared. Jokob stood behind Clayton, his hands raised in a question.

"Sorry, am I interrupting something? Should I wait downstairs?" Jokob shifted from one foot to the other.

Julianne allowed the door to swing open the rest of the way. "Not at all." She crossed her arms over her chest and gave Clay an annoyed look that left no doubt he needed to leave.

"Sure, sorry. Aren't you going to introduce us?" Clayton stumbled over his feet as he reached out his hand toward Jokob.

At the risk of coming off like a total bitch, Julianne replied, "I hadn't planned on it. Clayton, this is Jokob. Jokob, this is my ex-husband Clayton…who was just leaving."

Julianne stepped back and gestured for Jokob to enter, saying, "Good bye, Clayton." She closed the door, leaving Clayton standing in the hallway. "I'm so sorry you had to witness that." She paced across the floor in front of the door, talking with her hands. "He hasn't stopped by since our divorce and he picks *today* to do so? What was he thinking?"

"We can do this another time if you'd rather."

"No, I'm okay, he surprised me is all. I thought it was you at the door."

He smiled, his dimples peeking through. "You look nice. I wish I had my camera to capture what that blue does to your eyes."

Julianne blushed and picked up her shoulder-sweater. "It's always too darned cold in restaurants."

"Shall we?" Jokob extended his arm for her and they took the stairs out to his jeep.

"Good thing you put the top up. I heard it might rain."

He unlocked and opened the door for her. Julianne smiled. *It's been forever since anyone's been sweet to me.*

"Where to?" Jokob asked, as he climbed in and started the engine.

"I'll guide you. Take a left at the light. We're going to Rigazzi's. It's the oldest restaurant on The Hill, owned by the same family since 1957. My poppy is a nephew of the owner and a cousin of the Maitre d'. Come to think of it, I'm pretty sure everyone on The Hill is at least somehow related." Julianne laughed, knowing it was most likely true. "It's a very close-knit area full of restaurants, ranging from inexpensive family joints to expensive 4-star fine dining."

Julianne pointed. "Go over the highway and take the first right." She continued her story. "My poppy worked there as a teen, when he wasn't working for his own poppy."

"Your poppy?"

"Oh, sorry, my father, Giorgio. Poppy is an Italian term of endearment for father. Even though I'm a grown woman, he's still my poppy. We're very close."

"I can see I'm in for a bit of an education tonight."

Julianne directed him to a parking place along the street. She half-opened her door, but stopped as Jokob came around to her side. *This may take some getting used to, but I think I could definitely like it.*

They'd barely made it through the door before a very excited older man with wild, white hair rushed up and hugged Julianne. "My *bellacito*, why didn't you tell me you were coming? I would have saved your poppy's table for you."

Julianne smiled a smile that would melt butter. "Vincenzo, this is my friend Jokob O'Callaghan. He's a photographer in town doing some exhibits."

Vincenzo eagerly took Jokob by the shoulders and kissed him on both cheeks. "Any friend of my beautiful God Daughter is welcome. Please, come, sit."

Vincenzo led them to a table with a view of the fireplace. He called to a nearby waiter, "Antonio, vino for our friends," and clapped his hands enthusiastically. "I'll leave you two. You need anything, you let me know."

Jokob grinned at Julianne. "Wow, you really *are* family. Vincenzo is your… godfather?" he asked, lifting one eyebrow with a sideways tilt of his head.

"I guess that does sound a little funny. He actually is my spiritual god father, not like in the movie."

Antonio brought over a bottle of Chianti and two glasses. "A bottle of your poppy's best."

With practiced skill, Julianne inspected the bottle and cork. Antonio poured a small amount, which she swirled and tasted like a pro. She signaled to him that it was acceptable, and he poured a glass for each of them before retreating.

Julianne lifted her glass. "To new adventures."

Jokob clinked her glass, never once turning his gaze away. "Your poppy's wine? It's quite good. More of a beer man myself, but certainly appreciate good wine."

"My poppy is the vintner at The Villa Winery. He followed in his poppy's footsteps but makes the wine instead of distributing it like his poppy did. I suppose wine is the family business. My brother George also works at The Villa."

Antonio returned with menus, freshly baked bread, and dipping oil. Julianne caught the sparkle in his eyes as he grinned at them.

"So, what's good?" Jokob asked, and perused the menu.

"Everything is excellent, but you can never go wrong with the Cannelloni. It's a guarded secret recipe straight from the owner's mama's mama from Sicily."

"Well, how could I possibly pass that up? Cannelloni it is," Jokob said, closing his menu.

"I sure hope you're hungry," she giggled, signaling to Antonio. "Come." Julianne held out her hand. "Let me show you around while we wait."

Julianne led Jokob by the hand on a tour, stopping at various pictures to tell him some of the history of The Hill and the restaurant. As they headed back to their table, Jokob placed his hand lightly on the small of her back, sending electric tingles up and down her spine. She sucked in her breath and let it out slowly.

They talked all during the meal, laughing, sharing bread, wine, and savoring Cannelloni. Julianne had never felt so much at home with anyone. "It's so easy to talk to you. I usually have trouble with people I don't know well."

Jokob reached across the table and took her hand in his. "You're glowing with beauty. I haven't enjoyed myself this much in... well, a very long time."

Julianne buzzed with excitement. She imagined Vincenzo on the phone excitedly telling her momma and poppy that their *Tesoro* was out with a handsome man.

Antonio appeared at their table. "Shall I bring more wine?"

"Oh, no." She raised her eyebrows and shook her head laughing. "One bottle is plenty."

"You must have dessert."

Julianne smiled at Jokob. "You haven't lived till you've tasted their cannoli."

Jokob thumped his full belly, like it was a ripe melon. "I think I can squeeze in a little more."

After Antonio brought the cannoli, Jokob took a bite. "Oh my gawd, you weren't kidding. This is amazing!" Filling oozed onto his lips with his second bite.

Julianne laughed, reaching over to wipe off a smudge of filling.

The cannoli gone, Jokob signaled Anthony for the check and paid. "Shall we?" He stood and offered Julianne his hand.

He once again placed his hand on her back, as they strolled to the door, sending continued shock waves through her body. As they left the restaurant, he took her hand in his. "Would you like to walk a while?"

Julianne intertwined her fingers with Jokob's, luxuriating in their warmth.

They strolled through the neighborhood hand-in-hand, nowhere to be, and in no hurry to get there. *This is glorious.* Numb for so long, Julianne felt herself coming back to life.

"Was that a raindrop?" Julianne asked, holding her hand to the sky.

"I didn't feel anything."

A drop hit her square in the eye and Julianne giggled. "Now I know I felt that one."

Scattered drops developed into a steady onslaught. With shrieks of laughter, they raced toward the Jeep. They'd gone only a few steps when the skies opened up and the drops became buckets, drenching them to their skin. They jumped in soaked but laughing. Jokob reached behind the seats for towels.

"Would you like to come up?" Julianne asked, as Jokob maneuvered the Jeep into a parallel parking spot in front of her apartment.

"I was hoping you'd ask."

The rain had stopped. Jokob came around to open Julianne's door, which she'd left closed this time. He laced his fingers through hers on the walk up to her building and the single flight of stairs.

Julianne unlocked her door, feeling Jokob's hot breath on the back of her neck. He nuzzled her, one hand on each of her hips. Slipping inside, she closed the door. He pressed her lightly against the door and kissed her. The passion they'd each kept locked away broke free and gentle kissing became intense and breathy.

Julianne wondered how far this might go, when Jokob suddenly stopped kissing her, his lips hovering over hers. Holding his hands out in front of him, he backed away.

"I… I can't do this," he stammered. "I need to go." Jokob's face contorted with anguish and he reached for the doorknob.

"It's okay, we can stop. You don't have to leave, we can just talk."

"No. I need to go." Jokob grabbed the doorknob but turned back to Julianne with tear-laced eyes. "I really like you, but I'm…" He slowly shook his head. "I'm not ready."

Then he was gone.

Julianne locked the door and stayed with her hand on the knob until it grew warm beneath her touch, pondering what had just happened. *What must he be going through? What did someone whose spouse died do with their grief? Will he ever be ready?* With a heavy sigh, she finally released the knob and headed to her bedroom. She glanced at her cell phone. *Damn, it's too late to call Bella tonight… I'll call her tomorrow.*

eighteen

*L*ost in thought, Julianne stared out the hospital window, her shift almost over. *Will I ever hear from him again? It's been five days.* As she returned to the nurse's station to wrap up her duties before the shift change, her phone vibrated. It was a text from Jokob.

"Can you come to my RV tomorrow morning—10ish? Something I need to show you. I can fix lunch."

Julianne texted back, "Yes, I'll be there. Where is 'there?'"

"KOA historic Route 66, past Six Flags. Site 122."

After signing out of work, Julianne headed home. *I wonder what he needs to show me.* She heated her momma's leftover homemade chicken noodle soup and ate in front of the TV, trying to focus on the news, but unable to keep her mind engaged. Although she thought she wouldn't be able to sleep due to anticipation, she was beat after a four-day rotation and fell asleep within minutes.

Julianne woke with a start, looked at her clock. "Oh shit! I'm gonna be late!" She'd overslept. It was at least a half hour drive with no traffic, and she'd be right in the middle of rush hour. She texted Jokob, "Sorry, overslept and may be late. Need shower before I head over. Is that OK?"

Jokob texted back, "No problem… take your time."

She threw a coffee-pod into the maker and headed for a quick shower. After dressing in blue jean shorts, a red, sleeveless button-up shirt, and sandals, she glanced in the mirror and fluffed her curls again. She poured the coffee into her mug and raced out the door. Thirty minutes after waking, she was in her Prius heading to Highway 44.

Luckily, the traffic wasn't bad and she made good time, pulling up at Jokob's RV a few minutes before ten. She paused in the car, collecting her thoughts, before getting out and knocking on the door.

Jokob answered immediately. "Thanks for coming. I wouldn't have blamed you if you'd said no way after how I behaved the other night."

Julianne studied the man standing before her. His hair stuck out in all directions, and pale, dark bags painted the skin under his eyes. *Has he slept at all?* "Well, I was wondering if you'd ever call me again. I wasn't sure what had happened the other night." Julianne entered the RV and placed her purse on the table.

"Coffee?" he asked, gesturing toward a pot on a tidy counter.

"Gawd yes, only had time for one cup, and truth be told, I need two to be fully conscious and functional."

"How do you take it?"

"Sugar and lots of cream. Real, if you have it." She allowed her gaze to drift without turning her head.

"Please make yourself at home."

While Jokob busied himself with the coffee, Julianne roamed the sparse living space. "Wow, you live here?"

"Yup. Home sweet home for three years. I bought this RV shortly after Keara died. I hit the road and haven't been back east since."

Julianne shook her head, smiling slightly. Quiet scratching at the door interrupted them.

"I hope you like dogs." Jokob stopped mid-pour and opened the door.

The oddest dog Julianne had ever seen stepped through. Scruffy hair stuck out on his face and legs, but lay smooth on his back. His face was brown on one side, white on the other, with a pure black circle around that eye. He had one brown ear and one black ear. His back and one leg were a beautiful merle, and three of his legs were white with black spots, like a Dalmatian. His tail was black with a white tip and he had one blue eye.

"Who's this?" Julianne asked. The thigh-high dog sauntered over and nudged her hand for a pat, like they were old friends.

"That is my traveling companion, Cooper. I found him in Cooper City, Florida, hence the name. He was on the side of a dirt back road fighting vultures for carrion. Skin and bones, covered in fleas and ticks, but he didn't run when he saw me. Instead, he walked right up and sat down in front of me, like he's doing with you, and nudged my hand. So I made a deal with him. Told him he could come along, and I'd take care of him if he promised to be a good dog. That was about two years ago, and he's been a great dog. He even let me give him a good scrubbing and flea treatment. He never runs off, although I allow him to roam free when it's safe. He pretty much stays close to the RV."

"He looks like he got a piece of four or five different breeds, all in their own unique positions on his body," she said, ruffling him behind the ears.

Several framed pictures lined a small shelf across the room. "Are those your folks?" She gestured to a photo of an older couple.

Her attention diverted, Cooper swatted her hand with his paw. "You've got to watch out. He's got a mean right-hook," Jokob warned.

"Okay, okay, I get it." Julianne returned to her assigned duty as ear and belly rubber.

"Maternal Grandparents." Jokob picked up the photo, handing it to her. "They emigrated from Poland while my grandmother was pregnant with my mom. My dad's grandparents came from Ireland during the potato famine. I'm named after my paternal grandfather. My nickname growing up was Joko."

"Joko? I bet you got lots of ribbing as a kid." She giggled and couldn't help but stare at the cute dimple that peeked out from under his reddish beard when he grinned.

"And that one?" She pointed at the picture next to his grandparents.

"Parents. They still live in Cape Cod. Dad fishes, and Mom runs a little boutique on the bay that's mostly seasonal."

Julianne released herself from Cooper's demands for a closer look at the picture of a storefront decorated in the colors of the sea. She browsed the array of family photos, deciding there was much more to this man than good looks and talent.

Jokob brought her a cup of coffee and gestured to the couch. Once seated, he took her hand. "Julianne, I'm sorry for running off the other night. I thought I was ready. I wasn't prepared to feel what I was feeling. It scared me. Terrified me actually. I'm still damaged goods from Keara's death. I shut myself off from so many of my feelings, and they all rushed out at once. I felt like I was drowning, and I had to get away fast."

"I understand. I mean I understand you needing to get out. I can't really say I understand what you must be going through. I have no frame of reference for anything like that."

Jokob reached over and picked up something from the side table. "This is what I needed to show you." He handed Julianne a small, worn, lavender envelope with the words 'My Beloved' on the outside in deep purple calligraphy.

"Keara died shortly after she wrote this. I've never shown it to anyone… until now. I think you'll understand why I'm showing it to you once you've read it."

Julianne's hands shook as she opened the envelope and removed a single sheet of lavender paper, a slight lavender scent fluttered past her nose.

> *In the misty hour before dawn*
> *I lay awake listening to you breathe.*
> *We are snuggled tightly together*
> > *No space between, our arms and legs inter-*
> > *twined like our hearts.*
> *I shall miss you, My Beloved, but I must go soon.*
> *I know you'll miss me,*
> > *But do not linger and languish.*
> *Do not die in your heart.*
> *Begin again.*
> *Live again.*
> *Find the Jewel that will shine new light*

into your broken and bruised heart.
She'll need you as much as you'll need her.
The bridge will lead you to the Jewel.
She awaits.
Create new life with her.
I will always be a wisp of wind through the trees.
And the sunrise at dawn.

After wiping her tears to keep from wetting the paper, Julianne reread the poem. "I've never read anything so beautiful, so sad, and yet so full of promise."

"This poem is why I invited you to the sunrise bridge shoot. I don't believe in fate or destiny, but when I met you at the exhibit, I knew I had to find out. I had to know if you were the Jewel I was supposed to find. I kept wondering how she knew." Jokob's eyes brimmed, a tear escaped and rolled down his face. He again reached for Julianne's hand and searched her face.

"Wow. My nonna called me Jewel." Julianne shook her head in disbelief.

"After Keara died, the idea of opening my heart to someone new," he shook his head, "was something I knew would never happen. How could I expect to find another love as perfect for me as she'd been? Most people struggle to find one perfect love, but two? I didn't believe it was possible. And, quite frankly, I didn't want it to be. I never wanted to risk feeling pain like that again. And I didn't want to love if it couldn't be just as amazing."

Transfixed by Jokob's gaze, Julianne held her breath, not wanting to move lest she break the spell.

"I've met hundreds of women at my exhibits, many quite obvious in their desire to take me home. I never gave any a second thought, except as customers to buy my photographs. None sparked even the remotest interest."

Jokob looked down at his hands and back up, directly into Julianne's eyes. "Until you."

Cooper snuggled his snout under Jokob's hand.

"The other night at your place, I felt… " A heavy sigh escaped his lips. "Alive. That scared me and I ran. I needed time to think about what it meant and time to deal with the guilt for feeling those feelings, like I was cheating on my wife. I know, I know, she's gone. And I know she wanted me to move on. But it still felt wrong somehow." Jokob leaned back on the couch and sighed again.

Jokob faced Julianne. "You should know something about me. I don't do casual romance. Either I'm in, or I'm not, nothing in between. Over the past few days, I've also come to realize that I wanted to give you time to figure out if you want this too."

Julianne remained still, feeling the warmth from Jokob's hand, her heart and mind a tumble of thoughts and emotions. She reached out and stroked his cheek. Leaning in, she kissed him gently. She laid her forehead on his and whispered, "Yes," drawing the word out to a quiet hiss.

Jokob returned her kiss with light brushes across her lips. Pulling away, he jumped to his feet, smiled and held out his hand. "There's a lot you don't know about me, and a few things you must before you can truly say yes. But first, I'm starving. Would you like some lunch?"

"I thought you'd never ask. I didn't have breakfast and I thought the rumbling of my stomach must be drowning out all other sound. I was sure you could hear it."

Jokob laughed. "Maybe a little."

"Ahk!" Julianne threw a pillow at him.

Jokob headed for the kitchen, only a few steps away in the RV. "You like turkey and swiss? I bought some panini and deli meat at Trader Joe's. I have one of those cookers that grills them up nicely.

"Sounds yummy."

Jokob pulled the cooker out from the cabinet under the stove, gathered the bread and other fixings, and prepared lunch. Julianne watched his every move, thinking he looked as comfortable in the kitchen as he did behind a camera. *I guess he had to learn how to cook after Keara died.*

"You like Mayo? I've also got lettuce and tomato."

"Yes to all. Anything but onions and mustard. Can I help with anything?"

"Sure. There's a pitcher of sun tea in the fridge. You could get that and some glasses and take them out to the table." He pointed to the door. "It's gorgeous so I thought we could eat outside… if that's okay."

"Good." Julianne found two glasses, filled them with ice, and carried everything out.

When she returned, Jokob directed her to a cabinet. "Chips are in there. Pick what you like."

He shut off the cooker, slid a sandwich onto each plate, and headed out the door.

They took opposite sides of the picnic table. When she bit into her sandwich, the bread crunched and the cheese oozed out the sides. "Oh wow. I have *got* to get me one of those cookers. This sandwich is delicious."

"It helps to use the best ingredients also. I try to buy organic and sustainably raised when I can."

Julianne looked around at the other campsites, many empty. Quiet and peaceful. The few occupied sites seemed to be inhabited by older couples. "Is it always like this? When you're on the road?"

"What do you mean?"

"So still."

Jokob laughed and poured himself more iced tea. "It's only quiet here because school hasn't let out yet. In a few weeks, this place will be swarming with kids. I try to stay at family-oriented campgrounds. Less likely to have wild, loud parties until all hours of the night than some of the camps geared toward twenty-something's."

He wiped his hands and mouth and rolled up the bags of chips. "Don't get me wrong, I like a party as much as the next guy, but I often get up before dawn—"

Julianne's laughter interrupted him. "Yeah, I know."

"Right. Well, I can't handle a party every night. I stayed at a place a couple of years ago and didn't check out the grounds beforehand. Man, was that ever a mistake. I had to move after the second night."

Julianne reached over and took his hand. "What's been your favorite place?"

Jokob drew quiet and stared over Julianne's shoulder, as if looking for something far in the distance. For a moment, he seemed to drift away. "I think I'd have to say this little place down in the Florida Keys. Way down near the end in Boca Chica. We didn't stay long, but while we were there, man, talk about sunrises and sunsets. We could see both from our camper. When we weren't drawing, writing, or taking pictures, we spent hours walking the shoreline and snorkeling."

"Sounds lovely. I'd love to go there sometime."

"You should." He left it at that, not committing to taking her to a place he'd shared with Keara.

Jokob took her hand. "Come on back in. I've got something else to show you."

Once back inside the RV, Jokob strode the two steps across the RV to the family photos. "This," he said, handing her the photo, "is Jokob the fourth—sixteen on his next birthday. That's how old I was when he came to be."

Julianne's eyes widened, her mouth dropped. "You have a… " She gulped. "A son." More acknowledging a statement of fact than an actual question, it was a way of rendering it true by speaking it. She took a deep breath and released it.

"At sixteen I was pretty cocky. I was a star on the football field, and I'm told the girls thought I was pretty cute. I don't know about all that, but still." Jokob winked at Julianne and continued, "I could have about any girl I wanted, and as much as I hate to admit it, I had more than my share. But there was this one girl, Mary Beth, who didn't even seem to know I existed. Of course, that made me try like a dog after a squirrel to get her attention. It became a conquest. Damn she was hot, but in an understated, bookie kind of way, or maybe she was hot because I wanted her and couldn't seem to get her. Anyway, she finally agreed to go out with me. She surprised me by suggesting we go to the local make-out spot. I didn't think she even knew about the place. We'd been there less than five minutes when she jumped into the backseat and stripped. I followed right behind her, never one to turn a girl down."

Jokob paused and looked directly at Julianne. "Keep in mind that was me at sixteen, I've changed since then. I thought we were careful, but six weeks later, she calls to tell me she's pregnant, and that it's mine. Turns out, I was her first and only—she'd been a virgin before that night. The way she attacked me, I couldn't tell. I offered to do the right thing and marry her, even though I didn't even know her, but her parents refused to allow it. They were devoutly religious so abortion was out. So after much screaming and blame-throwing, both sets of parents decided we would all raise the baby together."

"Wow, I don't even know what to say, Jokob. What did your parents do?"

"They were pissed. Asked me if I was deliberately trying to screw up my life. But it was less about me, and more about them. You see, Dad had big political plans and this rocked his ambitions boat. He was on the city council at the time, with his sights set on mayor. He used the whole thing as sort of publicity campaign thing—you know, learn from his mistakes and work to prevent teen pregnancy. I was livid that he would use me this way, but somehow he twisted it to his advantage and got elected."

Jokob paused and got another glass of tea, offering more to Julianne.

She thrust out her glass. "I can see I'm going to need all the brain power I can get."

As he poured, she continued. "What happened to the baby?" Julianne traced her fingers across the photo of a young man, who passed for a younger version of Jokob—same reddish brown curly hair, deep crystal-green eyes, similar muscular build and same deliriously cute dimples.

"Mary Beth moved in with an aunt in another town and attended an elitist preppy school with a high percentage of pregnant teens. I know that sounds old-fashioned, but her parents insisted on it so she could continue to focus on her studies without other kids making fun. This girl was smart, I mean 4.0 plus smart, and they weren't going to let a little thing like a baby derail her from her dreams of becoming an astrophysicist. When she returned, we learned she'd named the baby Jokob. My dad hit the roof, said Jokob was a family name, and she had no right. It was intended for a 'legitimate heir.' He threatened to cut off financial support if she didn't change it. Mary Beth and her parents stuck to their guns and told Dad they'd take us all to court if he stopped supporting the baby. Breach of contract her lawyer dad said. Dad couldn't bear any negative publicity, so, the name Jokob stuck and he became 'the fourth.'"

Jokob took a big breath and let out a heavy sigh. "The name argument didn't make things any easier, but I was determined that my kid would know me. I spent as much time with him as Mary Beth would allow, always supervised because she considered me a bad influence." He glanced up at Julianne with a sheepish grin. "I'll tell you that story another time."

Julianne raised an eyebrow at that comment, but she could tell he had more to say, so kept she quiet.

"Even though Keara and I were on the road a lot, we made sure to spend time with little Joko when we weren't… until Keara died and I left. Now he joins me on the road during the summer. In fact, he was with me for a month down in New Orleans, right before I came here. I miss him, but he should be with his mom and friends, especially now that he's in high school."

Jokob popped to his feet. "I need a break. Don't run off while I'm gone, Okay?" Jokob backed toward the hall, winking at Julianne before he stepped into the bathroom.

Julianne glanced up from the framed pictures to find Jokob watching her. He came over and wrapped his arms around her waist. "Do you have to work tomorrow?"

"No, I'm off for a few days. What time is it?" Julianne asked, searching for her phone. She hadn't worn a watch since suffering a compound wrist fracture in a roller-blade accident in high school—the pressure of the band on still numb skin felt too weird. She wore a pendant watch around her neck for work.

"About four o'clock." Jokob led her over to the couch and invited her to sit. He pushed a curl behind her ear and asked, "Would it be too presumptuous of me to ask you to stay the night?"

Julianne chewed her thumbnail, torn between wanting to stay but not wanting to rush things.

"I don't know." She lifted her eyebrows and sucked her lower lip. "I have cats."

"I've heard cats can take care of themselves for a few days. Besides, it's almost rush hour." Jokob took her face in his hands, brushed his lips across hers and whispered, "Staaayyy."

All her resolve broke.

nineteen

*J*ulianne awoke to the smell of coffee and bacon, wearing the t-shirt Jokob loaned her. She'd been pleasantly surprised the night before when he told her he only wanted to sleep in her arms, that he wasn't ready to take it to the next level. They'd kissed, snuggled, and talked awhile before drifting off. She'd never actually fallen asleep in someone's arms before. She didn't think she would like it, but found that she did.

"Oh good, you're up," Jokob called out, when the creak of door hinges echoed through the RV. "Breakfast is almost ready."

Julianne admired the busy man in the kitchen—dark green cargo shorts, a multi-pocketed fishing shirt, and hiking boots. *Hmmm, now this I could enjoy waking up to every morning.*

Freshly squeezed orange juice already sat on the table and bacon sizzled in the pan, the smell permeating the small space.

"How do you like your eggs? Wait, you *do* like eggs, right?" Jokob asked, raising his eyebrows.

"Anything but poached. You know a girl could get used to this treatment." Julianne slipped up behind him, wrapped her arms around him, and rested her head on his muscled back. *Where have you been all my life?* She nuzzled him and purred.

Jokob shut off the stove and spun around to pull her into his arms. He placed his index finger on her chin and gently tilted her head for a morning kiss. "Ah, now that's more like it."

"It's ready, let's eat!" He patted Julianne on her backside and carried the skillet to the table. Julianne poured orange juice and coffee, and he dished out scrambled eggs, bacon, and toast.

"Dig in while it's hot," he encouraged.

I'll tell you what's hot— having a guy cook for me. She gazed seductively at Jokob.

Julianne took one bite of the eggs and exclaimed, "Oh wow, these eggs are amazing. How did you make them taste like this?"

"The secret starts with the egg itself. These are from local pasture-raised chickens eating what they're supposed to eat—bugs and such. I bought them from a farmer on one of my excursions, so they're super fresh. I add a bit of feta cheese shortly before they finish cooking, a little of my secret recipe seasoning, and that's it." With a flourish of his hands, he jumped to his feet and bowed.

"Secret seasoning, eh? You're too funny in the morning." He had her laughing all through breakfast. *I think I'm falling for this guy.*

When only breadcrumbs remained, Jokob cleared the table. They washed dishes together, standing hip-to-hip in the tiny space.

"How about another excursion today to Grafton? I read that the Grafton Ferry recently reopened after three years. It will give me a chance to explore some of the area where the river folk live. I've been told some of them are quite... colorful."

"That sounds like fun. I haven't ridden the ferry in years." Julianne stuck her nose under her arm and sniffed. "I guess my clothes aren't that dirty."

Jokob laughed. "I'll be the judge of that," he said, pulling her close, inhaling deeply.

There's that wink-grin again. Damn, does he have to be so cute all the time? I don't think I can resist this much longer.

"Go get dressed and let's get this day rolling. I'll map out the route."

He'd barely gotten the laptop booted up when Julianne appeared, dressed and ready. "Whoa, that was quick! Now I guess you'll just have to wait on me." His laughter bounced off the walls of the RV.

"Ha! Bet you thought I'd take forever. Well, the joke's on you, I'm not like most women." Julianne did a little mock curtsy, joining in the laughter. He brought out the mirth in her. It felt so much better than the dark and dreary place she'd spent the past year.

"No, you are certainly not like most women." Jokob stopped what he was doing and focused on her, his chin resting in his hand. He closed the laptop and scooped up his gear. "Let's go."

The day already promised to be sunny and warm. The route he'd selected took them through Old Town St. Charles and into the bottom lands. They drove through the cobble-stoned streets with the top off the Jeep, taking in the sights along the way.

Jokob pulled over for several photo opportunities. "I've learned that the best way to find hidden gems is to take my time, get off the beaten path. I'll want to go back into old St. Charles at some point while I'm here and check it out in more detail. I love quaint old-time areas. They have such character."

"There are some great places to eat around here—a micro-brew and a winery, too," Julianne offered.

"Are the people that live along the river really called River Rats? What do they think of that name?" Jokob asked, taking the last turn before the ferry.

"They're a tough bunch and actually like that name," Julianne explained. "The bottoms flood… a lot. But they stay put, rebuild when they have to. Many won't evacuate, which unfortunately puts a stress on the rescue resources. One year during a bad flood, a family refused to leave. The floodwater ate away the stilts and their house crashed into the river and floated downstream. Their five-year-old son was swept away and got lodged in a tree. When rescue workers arrived, he wasn't breathing, but they revived him and air-lifted him to my hospital's ICU. He later died from his injuries, along with one of the rescuers whose body was found fifty miles down river. Needless to say, the family was devastated. They lost their only child and their home. It was too much for them to think about rebuilding after that and they moved."

Julianne sipped her Dr. Pepper. "But for most, this is their life, and I suppose they love it in spite of the floods. Or, perhaps maybe because of them, and the challenge they present. I met this old guy who'd been brought into the ER after a flood. I'd gone to check on a friend and this guy called out to me from his curtained area. He was pretty messed up but told me that, when he's away from the river too long, something ached in his soul. He said the river water ran in his veins."

As they rounded the corner, Julianne gestured at the long line of cars stacked up to ride across. "Looks like everyone else had the same idea."

"Not a problem." Jokob eased the Jeep into line and put it in park.

"Here you drive," he announced, and hopped out.

"Wait, what? Where are you going?" Julianne protested, but shimmied over to the driver's seat.

"You *can* drive a stick?" Jokob grinned, pulled out his hand-held camera, and slipped a press pass lanyard over his head.

"Sure, Poppy insisted that my brother and I learn. But I'm really rusty, it's been years. Hope I don't mess it up." Suddenly inhibited, she wiped her sweaty palms on her shorts.

"You'll do fine. We've got maybe a half hour to wait, so I'm going to get some shots. You keep moving along in line, and I'll jump in when we're close."

He kissed her over the door.

Julianne tracked him as he worked, craning her neck to see around the other cars. He took pictures of cars, people in cars, the river, the birds, and the arriving and departing ferries. When he disappeared from her sight, she turned right and left, but couldn't find him. She settled into the seat and waited, inching forward when it was her turn.

After not seeing Jokob for at least twenty minutes, Julianne squirmed and fidgeted. As the last car before her crept up to the ramp, she twisted around, trying to locate him. *Come on, come on, come on.* She looked out the driver's window. The passenger door opened and the Jeep bounced when it closed. Startled, she jumped and squealed.

"Miss me?" he asked, leaning to give her a quick peck on the cheek.

"I was about ready to send out a search party. I don't know what I would've done if you hadn't shown up when you did." Julianne laughed and eased the Jeep onto the ferry for the short cruise into Illinois.

They spent most of the morning capturing images around the ferry landing and Grafton, continuing up the Great River Road to Pere Marquette Lodge for lunch. They ordered to-go boxes for a picnic and settled on a blanket under the trees overlooking the Illinois River.

"Last night you mentioned there were a few things I should know about you and told me about Jokob the fourth. What other deep dark secrets are you hiding under those cute dimples?" It was Julianne's turn to wink at Jokob.

"Remember the football accident I said led me to photography? That's only part of the story. After I broke my leg, I slid into a black hole emotionally. Seemed like everything I'd been living and working for was ripped from my grasp. I fell in with a bad bunch of guys—directionless, trouble-makers—you know the sort. I spent most of my time drunk and in fights—the principal and I were on a not-so-friendly first name basis. My buds, Marco, Jackson, Randy, and me were always cooking up some kind of mischief."

Jokob finished his lunch and lay on his back. "One night we decided it would be fun to break into the school. We poured soap into the air conditioning system—what

160

a mess. We started a couple of small fires and all the detectors shrieked. Just our luck, a patrol car rolled past as we bolted through the window. Bottom line, we got caught and ended up in the city jail."

Julianne listened intently, unable to imagine this sweet guy as that angry teenager.

"The other kids' parents' bailed them out, but oh no, not my dad. I was the mayor's son and he was going to make an example of me. I sat in the city jail for three days before I had a visitor. Coach paid my bail. He lingered to the side, while I gathered my belongings from the bailiff. His look said it all. The disappointment on his face cut me deeper than any tongue-lashing from my dad. He told me, 'Joko, I paid your bail, but you're not going home. Your dad agreed to me bailing you out on one condition. He said you couldn't go home until you straightened up. So you're coming home with me.' He didn't offer me a choice, and I knew better than to question him. We stopped at my house and got my stuff. I never lived with my parents again."

"Wow, your dad sounds like some piece of work."

"He has his moments. I settled into Coach's small attic room. That night at supper, he told me, 'Practice starts at eight—don't be late.'"

"I protested, 'But Coach, you know I can't play.'"

"'Don't matter,' he told me. 'You're still on the team, and that's that.' He pulled out the camera gear and told me to make myself useful."

"Coach saved me and led me to Keara, or at least the photography did."

Jokob took a deep breath, reached over, and took Julianne's arm. He pulled her down next to him. They stared into the cloudless blue sky as the occasional stray bald eagle danced on the air currents in the distance, too far away for Jokob to take pictures. Despite the warm pre-summer's day, a cool breeze wafted over them. Julianne snuggled in close and rested her head on Jokob's shoulder, her arm across his chest. For a time, they enjoyed the warm day and each other's arms.

"Did you ever reconcile with your folks? I can't imagine not being close to my momma and poppy. They are solid rocks in my life."

"I did, but it took a long time and Keara's intervention. That's another story." Jokob jumped to his feet. "Let's walk," he said, holding out his hand. They gathered the blanket, stowed it in Jokob's backpack, and strolled around the grounds of Pere Marquette Lodge.

"Hey, Keara, take a look at this," Jokob called down from the crest of the rise. The sun barely tickled the top edges of the trees as it approached sunset.

Julianne froze in her tracks.

"Hurry or you'll miss it," he called again, looking over his shoulder. She stared at him from the bottom of the hill. "What?" he asked. He shook his head and raised his hands in a shrug.

"You called me... Keara," she answered in a barely audible whisper, her throat clenched tight, as if a python had wrapped itself around it. She dropped her gaze to her shoes, afraid to look up, unable to move.

Jokob let out a short rush of air. "Julianne, I am so sorry." He half slid, half climbed down the hill to where she stood rooted to the ground.

"Maybe this is still too soon for you, it's really fast for me." She bent over with her hands on her knees, feeling like she'd been gut punched. Tears landed on her sandals.

Jokob sank to his knees. Placing his index finger under her chin, he lifted her face. He tenderly wiped away her tears and took her hand. Gazing into her eyes he said, "You know, I was married to my perfect mate for over ten years. I've barely looked at another woman, much less dated one, since."

He brushed the curls out of her face. "This is new to me. It's touching some raw places."

A cloud of intense sadness crept across Jokob's face. He moved to the woven blanket they'd spread out moments before and motioned Julianne to sit next to him. She remained standing, as if moving threatened her very existence. He pulled his knees up and wrapped his arms around them.

"Julianne, you need to understand something. I will always love Keara," Jokob said. "Can you ever really stop loving your perfect mate when they die? I never wanted to risk that kind of love again." He crawled to her and looked up into her tearful eyes. "Until I met you."

"But… " she said, standing and turning away from his gaze. "How do I compete with that kind of love… compete with a ghost?" She drew long, deliberate breaths, focusing on the shafts of dancing sunlight split by the trees as the sun continued its downward journey. The rustling leaves in the gentle breeze provided a melody that helped her focus on calming her emotions.

"You can't. And, you can't replace Keara. I hope you wouldn't want to try." He reached out his hand and tugged her down to the blanket. He guided her around to face him and stroked her cheek with the backs of his fingers.

"You can just be you, and I can just be me, and whatever we become together will be uniquely ours… will be," he wagged his finger between their chests, "us." The tears glistened on his cheeks, dampening his beard. "Julianne, I haven't felt this happy or alive in years."

Julianne pondered Jokob's words. Finally, she said, "You were blessed with such an amazing love." She gazed into those intense eyes, the gold flecks dancing with the fire of the setting sun. She also felt what she hadn't wanted to ever feel again. She leaned over and hugged him, resting her head on his chest for a moment.

Rising, she held out her hand to Jokob. "We should head back before we lose the light."

By the time they made it back to the lodge, the sun had set and only the final dim glow of dusk lit their path.

Jokob slapped what seemed like the hundredth vicious mosquito. "Damn! Are these bloodsuckers always this bad around here? The way they're attacking, you'd think I was a blood sandwich. Retreat's our only option."

"I don't know what's up. They don't usually bite me and they're eating me alive, too. If they're this bad now, it doesn't bode well for summer." Julianne slapped again.

They ran slapping and laughing through the entrance of the lodge, pulling the door closed behind them to prevent more from following them in.

Jokob twirled Julianne around once through the door. "I don't want this evening to end. Would you consider staying here with me tonight?"

Julianne smiled, tucking her chin and looking up through her lashes. "I'd like that. If you don't mind a stinky date tomorrow. These clothes will be on their third day."

"Yeah, I know. Phew." Jokob waved his hand in front of his face.

"What? You little—"

"Only kidding. You smell fine. I think I can survive it, if you can." Jokob stepped over to the counter and asked about a vacancy.

"We have one double queen room left, sir. It's $119 per night." The dainty night clerk looked to be about eighty—white hair with a hint of blue, skin like paper, and a radiant smile that leaked joy.

"We'll take it. Is the restaurant still open?" Jokob asked.

"Yes, until nine." She fiddled with the face on her watch, shifting her glasses. "It's only eight now, so you have time."

"Great." Turning to Julianne, he said, "I'm starving. We can go to our room after some food." Jokob extended his hand, and they headed off to the lodge dining room.

After dinner and wine, they strolled through the great lodge hall. They stopped to play chess on a giant game laid out on the floor. Looking up at the ceiling revealed rough planed logs for joists. They settled on the couch in front of the fireplace and watched the flickering flames, hearing the crackle as the fire warmed their faces.

Julianne raised her hand to her mouth to suppress a yawn.

"Tired of me already?" He winked again.

"I can't help it. It gets dark outside, I yawn. That's one reason I'm glad I'm done with the nightshift. It was brutal."

Jokob tilted his head and grinned, flicking a glance over his shoulder toward their room. "Let's go."

As soon as the door closed behind them, Jokob pulled Julianne close, kissing her with increasing urgency.

Julianne returned his kisses, becoming breathless as the heat escalated between them. But she pulled away, whispering, "We need to slow this down." She hopped onto the bed and patted it for Jokob to join her. "I think we've got some unfinished talking to do."

They piled all the pillows from the two queen-sized beds together onto one, kicked off their shoes, and snuggled fully dressed under the blanket.

"I wish I'd known Keara. Tell me more about her," Julianne said, taking his hand in hers. "How did you meet?"

"It was the start of my senior year. I'd picked up photography quickly—I guess I had a knack for it," he said, shrugging. "It's almost like it had been sitting there waiting for me to stop messing around with football and discover it. By that time, I'd graduated from taking football pictures to being the yearbook photographer, which meant being on the yearbook committee. I walked into the first meeting of the year, first period on a Tuesday, and there she was. Long bright red ringlet curls flowed over her shoulders and down to her waist, she looked like a goddess. No makeup—she didn't need any. Her complexion was pure creamy silk, with just the right smattering of light freckles. It was obvious she was in charge, and at first, she didn't even give me a second glance. Or so I thought. Turns out, she was simply shy and hyper-focused on the work. As soon as class let out, I asked her on a date. She shot me down so fast my head spun. Said she knew all about me and didn't go out with my type of guy. I tried to tell her that I'd changed—and I really had. Since Joko the fourth, and the arrest, I was no longer the hot dog of the school. I'd learned my lesson on both fronts. It took me a month of daily yearbook committee meetings before she finally agreed to a date, but only in a public place. We were together from that first date until her last breath."

Jokob paused and sucked in ragged breaths. "I haven't talked about Keara to anyone. I guess I felt it would be diminishing her memory to talk about her. For some reason it just feels right to share her with you."

Julianne gazed at him, her earlier hurt dissolving as he talked. But as he shared more about Keara, she felt the depth of his love. Her concern that it was too soon, that she was setting herself up for a major heartbreak, grew stronger.

"Meeting Keara probably saved my life. It certainly gave my life direction, meaning. I focused on my photography and gave thought to my future. I had no idea what I'd do after high school. I wasn't exactly college material. Lucky if I could hold a 2.0 GPA. Keara, however, knew her path was writing. Even before high school, her poetry had won awards, and been published. She planned to pursue a degree in Creative Writing at Columbia University in New York. She convinced me to apply as a conditional student and at least take a few courses. I agreed, and we moved to New York together. With classes that focused on fine arts instead of pure academia, school finally worked for me. The material felt useful. I learned a lot and my skills developed. With more photography skill, my confidence for the required academic classes also strengthened. I ended up earning a bachelor's degree in Fine Arts. A few days after our graduations in June, we married on the beach in Cape Cod.

"We both knew we wanted to travel, but weren't quite sure what that might look like. A tragedy helped decide it. A month after our wedding, Keara's dad was killed when a hit-and-run driver forced his bike off the road. He was only forty-two. He'd always planned to travel after retirement. Selling life insurance had been lucrative and he had tons of it so he left each kid a hefty inheritance. Keara and I decided to use the money traveling, since he never got the chance. We bought a truck and a pop-up camper, loaded what we needed, and stored the rest in her mom's attic. We agreed to spend no more than three months in any given spot. I would take pictures, she would write, and we'd figure out how to earn a living from it as we went."

Julianne stifled a yawn.

"I'm boring you, I knew it!" Jokob laughed, pulling Julianne to him for a kiss.

"No, I love hearing about your life. I want to know you."

"Well, OK, if you're sure it's not time for sleep." Jokob hopped up and grabbed a beer from the room fridge. "Want one?"

She shook her head. "I've never acquired a taste for beer. But I could use some water. Tap is fine."

He got a cup, removed the hotel condom from it, and returned with water.

"Traveling worked out beautifully. Seems we were both suited for that nomadic kind of life. We'd already decided we didn't want kids until our thirties. No kids, no pets, no house, no apartment—just open road. We traveled light—if it wasn't tiny, we didn't buy it. Our souvenirs were my photos, or t-shirts. God, I loved that life." Jokob took a long pull off his beer and stared at the wall.

"Keara published poems and short stories and a few of my pictures sold, so we had somewhat of an income and didn't need to dip too deeply into her inheritance. As time passed, we both improved on our art. I started holding exhibitions in the towns we visited. We did this for nine years." Jokob paused and met Julianne's gaze. "Are you sure you want to hear all this? It isn't pretty."

"Yes, I do." Julianne reached out, gently touching his arm, her emotions running on overdrive. Her throat tightened and her breath ran shallow, but listening was necessary for her to truly know him.

Jokob cleared his throat. "We were in Denver when the bottom dropped out of our world. It started out as a good thing. Out of the blue, Keara's pregnant. We weren't planning it, it just happened and we were over the moon happy. We decided we would go to Seattle for my friend, Kevin's, wedding, stay a while, and take a long slow trip across the northern states back to Cape Cod. She wanted to spend her third trimester with her mom and sisters and be there when the baby was born.

"To make sure everything was going well, Keara made an appointment with an OB in Denver. That's where we were closest to at that time. The OB found the lump. Ironically, it was because of her pregnancy that they found it. I mean, at thirty-one, who even checks for breast cancer, right? The OB sent us to The University of Colorado Cancer Center. The pregnancy had amped it up like steroids, and she was already stage four—it had spread to her liver and spine. We headed straight back to Cape Cod…"

twenty

Keara
... three years earlier

K eara's hand trembled as she dialed the phone. "Mom? Um, would you mind if Jokob and I came home for a while?"

"Of course not, honey," her mom replied. "Is everything alright, dear?"

Keara struggled to maintain composure. She didn't want her mother to stress about this before she had to. "We can talk about it when we get there. We'll be there in three days."

"Ok honey, be safe."

Keara hung up and looked down at her shaking hands.

The sun still lingered on the horizon when they arrived at the family home on the southern end of Cape Cod. Jokob pulled the truck and camper onto the side drive. Keara's mom and Tim, her live-in boyfriend of two years who Keara had only met a few times, greeted them on the walk in front of the house.

All the fear and tension from the past week burst like a damn as soon as Keara saw her mom. She threw herself into open arms. "Mommy," she wailed.

Perplexed, Tim looked toward Jokob. Jokob gave a slight shake of his head and squeezed his eyes tight.

Her mom shepherded Keara into the kitchen. "Here, honey. Sit down and tell me what's wrong."

Tim hovered behind her mom's chair, resting his hands on her shoulders. Jokob slipped into the chair next to Keara and clasped her hand.

Keara sobbed, her shoulders heaving. She took a few deep, slow breaths and tilted her face toward the ceiling. When she looked back down, she met her mother's gaze. "Mom, I have cancer."

Her mom gasped, putting her hand to her mouth.

"And, I'm pregnant."

Her mom lowered her hand, her jaw slack. "How far along? And what kind?"

"About nine weeks." Keara scrunched her mouth to the side, and pinched her lips together trying to decide how to tell her. She decided that blunt was best. "Breast cancer. Stage four. It's already in my liver and spine."

Her mom wailed, "Oh God, no. No. No. No." She squeezed her eyes tightly, shaking her head with each no.

Tim tightened his grip on her shoulders. Her mom reached up and grabbed his hand.

Jokob finished the story for Keara. "They found it when she went into Denver to have the baby checked out." His voice came out thin and low. "It was supposed to be a routine OB visit."

Her mom shuddered and reached out a hand to pat Keara's. "What about the baby?"

Keara's tears began fresh. She whipped her head side-to-side. "I… I can't talk about this right now."

Her mom stumbled around the table and took Keara into her arms, rocking her back and forth. They cried until there were no more tears, and only exhaustion remained.

"I think we should all get some rest. I'll call Dr. Henry in the morning."

The appointment was set before Keara and Jokob came out of their bedroom at nine.

"Dr. Henry can see us at ten this morning. We'll need to leave soon to get there in time. I made egg sandwiches, so we can all eat on the way."

"Mom, I… " Keara stopped herself. It would do no good to argue. Although she appreciated everything her mom did for her, and certainly for what she was likely to do over the next few months, Keara grew resentful; she was doing it again. She was only happy in control, regardless of the situation. During the wedding planning, her mom had taken charge to the point they'd come to harsh words. The wedding her mom wanted for her was not the one Keara wanted. Though they'd managed to work out their differences, and had compromised on some details, it had carved a rift between them. Keara couldn't use any of her limited energy fighting with her now.

Her mom drove, leaving Tim at home. They arrived at the oncologist's office shortly before the appointment time. Keara glanced furtively around the office. It was much like the one in Denver. *How depressing.* She avoided making eye contact, not wanting the fear that enveloped the room to seep into her more deeply than it already had.

Keara's hand shook as she completed the paperwork. When she got to the question 'Are you pregnant?,' she inhaled sharply. She tilted her head back and looked up at the ceiling, fighting the tears. Once she completed the paperwork, she handed it to the receptionist and sat to wait.

And wait, and wait. Over an hour after they arrived, the nurse called her back. Her mom insisted on going in with them.

Dr. Henry came in before they'd settled in the chairs all arranged in a semi-circle on one side of an enormous mahogany desk. He reached out his hand to Keara. "I'm so sorry for your wait."

He shook Jokob's hand. "It's the nature of this specialty. I spend as much time with each patient as needed and that sometimes pushes me behind schedule."

He stopped in front of her mom. "Nancy. It's been a long time. You're doing well I trust."

She rose and hugged him as only dear friends would. "I was until my daughter arrived home last night with this devastating news." She dabbed under the edges of her glasses with a tissue.

Dr. Henry took the fourth chair. "I spoke with Dr. Anthony. She gave me a run-down on your diagnosis and sent me your tests results electronically. I don't want to redo tests, you'll get enough as we go along. No need to burden your system any more than we have to."

"Thank you," Keara said, taking a deep breath, only realizing afterward that she'd been holding it.

"I want to get you started on chemotherapy and radiation as soon as possible, however, there is one thing. I know that Dr. Anthony advised you to abort your pregnancy—"

Her mom interrupted. "Keara? You didn't tell me this." She edged to the front of her seat and gripped the arms.

"Mom, I... " She clung to Jokob's arm.

The doctor looked from Keara to her mother before turning to Keara. "I know this is difficult, but I concur. We will be pumping you full of toxins so strong you will be fighting for your own life. There's little chance a fetus will survive, and it's a huge unknown as to what kind of damage it would suffer if it did. You need all your body's resources to fight for your life."

"No, I've made up my mind. I understand the risks, but if there's even a one percent chance my baby could survive, I have to take it. This may be my only chance to be a mother."

Her mom leaped to her feet. "Jokob, can't you talk some sense into her?"

Jokob simply stared at the floor. He had done his best on the three-day drive to persuade Keara, but she had refused, saying, 'How can I kill another human being to save myself? I can't, I won't.'

Dr. Henry reached out and placed a hand on Keara's knee. "Keara, it may be your only chance to survive. We can harvest your eggs and freeze them."

Keara clenched her jaw and glowered at the doctor through eyes raw from tears. She shook her head no.

Her mom glared at Keara, her eyes narrowed to slits. She whirled and stomped through the door, slamming it behind her, rattling the degrees on the wall.

Dr. Henry shrugged. "I'll call the treatment center and you should be able to go on over. It's in the building next door. We'll start with targeted radiation on your breast, liver, and spine. That will jump-start the cancer's death. I should warn you, the radiation will blister your skin, worse than any sunburn you can imagine. After that, you'll receive a triple cocktail—it's quite powerful… and toxic. You'll become sicker than you've ever felt. You'll come back each week for another round. After four rounds, I'll re-do the tests to see where things stand. Do you have any questions?"

Keara shook her head no again. Jokob stared straight ahead, his eyes glazed over.

Life as they knew it was over.

Keara pushed the front porch swing with her bare toes, hands resting protectively on her protruding belly. After four months of treatment, she was used to her baldhead. Today was a good day. The nausea and diarrhea from last week's treatment had finally eased. Vaping marijuana helped. *To hell with the law.* Today was test day and she needed to psych up for it. They were long and boring, and often painful. She feared nothing was working. The stabbing pain in her back steadily worsened, and at times, her legs failed her. In spite of everything, she was happy. Their baby had continued to grow. They hadn't killed it. Not yet at least.

Keara and Jokob waited in the doctor's office. Keara bounced her legs on her toes, and she chewed the inside of her lip while they waited.

Dr. Henry rushed in and pulled up a chair. "I have good news, okay news, and… " He looked away. "The mets in your liver have shrunk considerably. The mets on your spine aren't shrinking, but they aren't growing, either. However… " The doctor shuffled in his chair and pretended to read the paper in front of him.

The smile on Keara's face fell. "However?"

"I'm afraid I have more bad news. The cancer has spread since the last test. There are now mets in your bones and brain."

Keara inhaled swiftly, her gaze flitted around the room. She squeezed her eyes tight, her legs continuing to bounce wildly.

Jokob said, "How is that possible? You're giving her enough drugs to kill a whale."

"This is how it often goes when a diagnosis is made at stage four. There's already so much cancer in the system the amount of drugs needed to kill it would also kill the patient."

Jokob jumped up. "The patient? This is my wife we're talking about."

"I know, I'm sorry," he said, swallowing hard. "I don't tell many patients this, but I've been in your shoes. I lost my youngest sister five years ago. She was only forty-two. I don't tell you this for sympathy. I tell you this so you know that I truly do understand your frustration."

Jokob fell into the chair and dropped his head into his hands.

Keara stopped bouncing her legs, lifted her head, drew her shoulders back and set her jaw. "What now?"

Dr. Henry sighed. "I… there is no what now. Your body isn't responding. There's nothing else we can do." He ran his hand over his mouth.

"I refuse to accept that. I'm six months pregnant. If you can't save me, you at least have to keep me alive long enough to give him a fighting chance."

"We don't even know if the baby is developing properly. You've refused ultrasounds."

"It doesn't matter, he's either fine or he isn't. Having an ultrasound won't change his outcome." She paused and simply blinked at the doctor. Finally, she asked, "How much time do I have if we stop treatment?"

Jokob grabbed her hand, shaking his head. "Keara. No."

Placing her palm on his face, she smiled into his eyes, willing hers to shine love. "My beloved, it's too late for me. There's nothing else he can do. All we can do now is hope our baby has a chance."

Her hand still on Jokob's face, she asked at the doctor. "How long?"

"It's hard to say. The brain met will be the most challenging. It popped up after the previous test so it's likely to grow quickly. You could have a few weeks, you could have a few months."

"All I need is a month." Keara rose, and held her out hand. "Sweetie, let's go home."

Five weeks later, Keara awoke unable to stand. Although her legs felt like rubber, pain shrieked through her, like blazing lightning. For the first time since her parents had it installed, she clicked the call button next to the bed.

Jokob raced up the stairs, yelling, "What?" He rushed to the bed.

Keara writhed in agony.

"It's time," she managed to say through clenched teeth.

Jokob was confused at first. The baby wasn't due for another two months. When he finally understood, his breath caught. They had agreed that when it got to the point where Keara was afraid she was dying, they would deliver the baby. Jokob swallowed hard, nodding his agreement. He called for an ambulance and let the delivery team know they were on their way.

By the time they arrived at the hospital, Keara was delirious from pain; her orders had been no pain medication because of the baby. Their prearranged plan was to attempt an epidural and deliver via C-section, so the baby wouldn't die with her. There was a chance it wouldn't work due to the spinal mets, but the OB had agreed to try. Keara feared if they knocked her out, she would never wake up.

The OB and neonatal team stood by prepped and ready and whisked Keara to the delivery room. The epidural worked, and within an hour, the baby was out. "It's a boy," the OB called out.

The room exploded into frenzied activity.

While the OB stitched Keara and pumped her full of Dilaudid, the neonatal doctor rushed the infant to the awaiting warming table. The plan was to transfer him to the NICU, but the doctor turned around instead and looked directly at Jokob.

Jokob froze.

Unable to see the doctor due to the surgical drape, Keara yelled, "Why isn't he crying? Is he alive? Is he OK? Somebody tell me something, damn it!" Keara screamed, crazy from pain.

"One moment." The neo doctor carefully wrapped the baby's head and swaddled it tightly. He placed him gently in Jokob's arms, held his gaze for a moment, and slowly shook his head.

Moving to the Keara's side of the drape, the doctor said, "I know you were both prepared for this possibility, but there's no still easy way to say this. Your baby has some severe," he said, looking down, "malformations. He most likely won't survive twenty-four hours."

Keara held out her arms. "Give him to me," she demanded.

Sobs racked Julianne's body.

Jokob stopped talking and paced around the room. "I was so angry with her for not aborting, because I needed her to live. But she was like that, headstrong when she'd made up her mind. A lot like her mother, but I would have never said that to her. I didn't have much choice other than to support her decision."

Jokob gaped at Julianne through a blur of tears. "He was beautiful. He had a head full of bright red hair, just like Keara's."

"We called Father Francis and with the family gathered in Keara's small hospital room, we had him christened. We named him Martin, after Coach. Everyone took turns holding him. He died in Keara's arms twelve hours after he was born."

He paused and met Julianne's gaze. "Keara died in mine three days later. I buried them together in the same coffin. I sold our camper and truck, bought the RV and a new Jeep, left Cape Cod, and haven't been back."

Jokob sobbed, too, dropping to the bed. Years of holding in grief broke free. Julianne pulled his head into her lap, stroking his hair while he cried. *This amazing, beautiful man has been through so much.* After Jokob fell asleep, Julianne lay down behind him and formed her body to his.

twenty-one

s soon as she was out of sight of Jokob's RV, Julianne punched up Bella's number on her cell. Bella answered on the first ring. "Hey girl, where've you been? I've been trying to reach you for two days. You aren't answering your phone."

"I've been with Jokob since Friday afternoon—"

"You go, girl!" Bella interrupted, excited. "So, tell me everything."

"He's amazing," Julianne said, but her voice wasn't convincing.

"But? You don't sound as thrilled as you should be if he's amazing."

Julianne paused, seeking to identify the feeling of dread that had been stalking her all day.

"I think I'm in love with him, but that's silly. I've only known him three weeks."

Between laughs, Bella said, "You've obviously forgotten who you're talking to. It's me, Bella… remember me? The girl who told you the night after my first date with Alessandro that I was going to marry him? I knew I loved him on that first date. So three weeks is plenty of time."

"I'm scared. He told me all about his dead wife. Bella, he's still in love with her. How do I compete with a ghost? Plus, he leaves for Seattle in two months. What am I supposed to do with that? I don't want to pull out all the stops and let myself fall head-over-heels only to have him leave, or worse, realize he isn't ready to love again." No longer able to fight the tears, Julianne pulled into a park-n-ride lot and burst into sobs.

Bella waited quietly for Julianne to get it out. "Jules, he will always love her. But give him the benefit of figuring out for himself if he can love again. And, if it's meant to be, and he feels the same way, a little thing like distance isn't going to matter. You'll work it out."

"You're probably right, but I can't help feeling like I should run now and protect myself. I'm gun-shy after what Clay did."

Julianne let out a heavy sigh. "Thanks for being there. I've really gotta hang up and drive. My shift starts in two hours, I need a shower, and I'm at least a half hour from home."

"Okay, call me if you need to talk or cry. I love you. Ciao."

twenty-two

*J*ulianne fidgeted at the nurses' station during her break. Despite the talk with Bella, she still felt conflicted. She liked Jokob, but she couldn't see how a future with him would work. She needed space and was glad she had four days before her next day off. Time to think. She also felt the need to tell Jokob what was going on with her, given everything he shared. She waited for noon to send an email, hoping he'd already be out in the field and not see it until later. Nervous he'd take it the wrong way, and not wanting to blow it, she nonetheless pressed send.

> *"Jokob, I had a really good time over the past few days. Thank you for sharing Keara with me. The depth of your love is something I aspire to.*
>
> *You know I'm working four 7-7's and can't see you, but I also need to tell you that I need this time, this space away from you, to think. I really like you, probably more than I should. But I feel like I'm heading for a fall since you're leaving in eight weeks. I feel like I need to protect myself so I'm not left here alone holding my bruised and bloodied heart in my hands when you drive away. So if I don't call you, it will mean I can't risk that kind of hurt, and just know that I've enjoyed being with you. Julianne"*

She answered a patient's call, but before she got ten feet, a reply came back. So much for hoping he wouldn't see it until later. She stopped and glanced at her phone.

> *"Julianne, I hear you and understand. I have similar feelings, but for me the biggest hurdle is allowing myself to fall in love again. I barely survived losing Keara and Martin. I couldn't survive another loss.*
>
> *But with that said, please don't write us off without talking to me first. If it's meant to be, and we both feel the same way, a little thing like distance isn't going to matter. We'll work it out. Jokob"*

Julianne took a deep breath and looked up at the ceiling to stop the stinging tears, remembering Bella had told her the same thing last night. She moved toward the patient call, emotions churning the bile in her stomach.

Julianne stared out the hospital window. The beginning of the sunset glinted on the horizon, her shift almost over. She turned to head back to her duties, and there he stood leaning on the wall, thumbs tucked into his pockets, watching her gaze at the sunset. He sauntered over, took her in his arms and kissed her with an urgency that made her knees wobble. He held her face in his hands and stared mesmerized into her eyes.

Without a word, he walked away, leaving Julianne standing at the window on shaky knees, her mouth agape, and her heart pounding.

Julianne's four-day workweek over, she was looking forward to three glorious days off. She dialed, hoping he'd answer.

"Hi, sunshine," Jokob said. "I was hoping you'd call. I'm sitting here outside my RV watching the most magnificent sunset. It has purple and pink streaks with orange splashes."

Julianne stopped and looked toward the west. "Oh wow, it's brilliant." She continued her walk home. "So look, I've decided I'm in, if you are. We can figure it out as we go, right?"

The silence that followed caused her heart to race. *Oh crap, he's changed his mind.*

"Jokob?" she asked, barely above a whisper, hoping that maybe the connection had dropped.

"I'm here. I needed a minute before I could respond." Jokob let out a slow breath. "Yes, we can figure it out as we go. I can't say I won't get spooked with feelings again, but what's life if you're not living it."

Julianne felt the corners of her mouth turn upward. "Whew. I thought I'd blown it. So I'm calling because my momma invited me to supper tomorrow night and she asked me to bring you. Apparently, Antonio from Rigazzi's has been talking to my poppy, telling him all about our date. I knew that wouldn't stay quiet for long."

"I would love to meet your parents and see where you grew up. What time should I pick you up?

"How about five? Oh, and my friends Bella and Alex will also be there with their two little ones, and our grocer, Marco and his wife, Fiorella, too. I hope you don't mind a full house of strangers."

"Your grocer?"

"Well, way more than that. He's also like a second father to me and a long-time friend of the family."

"I don't mind at all. More people for me to grill about you."

"Ha ha ha." But Julianne really was laughing. Light and free, feelings that, if she were honest, she'd been missing since long before Clay left.

The house was a din of chaos when Julianne and Jokob arrived. Nicky and Isabella played with Lego blocks on the dining room floor within view of their mother, who was in the kitchen talking a mile a minute and helping Julianne's momma, and Marco's wife, Fiorella. Her poppy, Alex, Marco, and her brother, George, sipped wine on the patio, their boisterous Italian trickling through the screened door.

"Momma, we're here!" Julianne called out from the living room, guiding Jokob toward the sounds.

"Jules! Come, come," her momma called back.

"Everyone, this is Jokob." Julianne beamed.

Bella squealed and ran around the bar counter. She swept Julianne into a hug, set her down, and spun to Jokob, hugging him. "Hi, I'm Bella. I'm the closest thing to a sister Jules has. Those two rug rats are mine."

"I'm Fiorella. I have grocery," she said from across the counter in broken English.

Her momma wiped her hands and came around too. "I'm Sibeal, Julianne's mother. I'm so delighted to finally meet you." She urged Jokob into a full hug.

188

"We're huggers in this family, better get used to it," she said, holding him out to take a better look. Winking at Julianne, she patted his chest.

Julianne watched, a grin pulling at the corners of her mouth. She'd been hoping her family would like him as much as she did. Tickled at how Jokob allowed this invasion of his personal space, she couldn't help feeling that something magical was happening.

Julianne tugged on Jokob's arm to extricate him from her momma's grasp and led him toward the backyard. "Let's go meet the rest of the family."

Exuberant Italian increased in volume as they neared the door. Her poppy rushed over, swooping Julianne into a bear hug, lifting her off the ground and spinning her around. "My *Tesoro mio*."

Her laughter rang clear as her feet settled back on the bricks. "Poppy, this is Jokob."

Her poppy released her and stuck out his hand toward Jokob. When Jokob accepted the hand, her poppy yanked him into a hug and squeezed. "This is the young man we've heard so much about?" He winked at Julianne.

Julianne pointed around the table. "Jokob, this is my brother, George. And Alex, or Alessandro, as Bella likes to call him. And Marco, the master of making my life simpler." She wagged her finger at all of them and said, "Now you guys be polite and speak English. We have a guest."

Patting him on the arm, she said, "Jokob, I'll leave you with the men. I'm going to go help with supper."

"What can I help with?" Julianne asked back in the kitchen.

189

"I like your young man." Her momma pointed to the chopping block. "Please make the salad."

"OMG," Bella giggled, "He's even cuter than I remember from the show. He's not just cute, he's hot."

"I know, right?" Julianne laughed. It felt good to be with family—to be happy. She wondered if perhaps the struggle of the past year was finally over.

The oven timer dinged and her momma pulled her signature Chicken Spedini and garlic bread from the oven. "Julianne, call in the boys. We're ready to eat."

While her momma, Fiorella, and Bella took the various dishes of food to the table, Julianne did as asked. As the dining room filled, the excitement amped up to a dull roar.

Bella settled Nicky in his booster seat before placing Isabella in her high chair and scooting into the chair next to her. Alex prepared a small plate of food for each of them and took the chair by Nicky. Julianne loved their routine, each dealing with one child.

Her poppy moved around the table, pouring wine, and took his place at the head of the table, with George at the other end. He stopped at Jokob's place and said, "This wine is from my private stock. I make wine for The Villa Winery, but also here in my basement. It's my job and my hobby."

Jokob took a sip. "A hint of pepper, vanilla, black cherry." He swallowed. "Hmm, chocolate on the finish. Superb. You made this?"

"Yes, I will show you the cellar later." Her poppy beamed.

"What varietal is this?" Jokob asked. "I don't think I've had it before."

"Norton. It's a Missouri native grape and is one of my specialties." Her poppy handed the bottle to Jokob.

"Julianne tells us you're a photographer?" her momma asked, clearing the salad bowls before serving the Spedini.

"Yes. I travel the country taking pictures. Sometimes I'm after a theme, such as sunsets. Often I work to capture the particular culture or vibe that makes any area or town what it is… its character. I've produced several books."

"You travel all the time? You don't have a home?" Her momma shot a sideways glance at Julianne.

"I live in an RV. I spend a few months at each place, and move on."

"And you like this? What about family?" Her momma pressed.

Jokob's jaw slackened and he lifted an eyebrow toward Julianne, who sensed his need for rescue.

"Momma, don't badger." Julianne shot her momma a stern look and changed the subject. "Our first date, well, it really wasn't a date, more like an outing. Anyway, it was to the Clark Bridge in Alton to take pictures of the sunrise. It's so peaceful there before the sun comes up."

"So George, what do you do?" Jokob asked.

"I'm the Grounds Foreman for The Villa. It's my job to ensure that the vines are properly cared for. Pruned, sprayed for bugs, mold, that sort of thing. I also manage the harvest each season so Poppy can make the wine. You should come out sometime. I'll show you around."

"That would be great. Would you mind if I took pictures?"

"Not at all."

191

"I can't even recall the last time I sat down for a family gathering. Being on the road makes it hard to do. Sibeal, thank you so much for including me."

Her poppy opened a third bottle and poured more wine. "So Jokob, where is home?"

"All over really. I was an Army brat. But my folks are now in Cape Cod."

"Are your parents well?" her momma asked under Julianne's warning glare.

"Yes, very, thank you."

Julianne ate and smiled as her family and friends welcomed Jokob warmly. She'd been concerned that they would be wary of letting a new man into their lives, after what Clay did. After all, he'd been their son for over four years. They had loved him and he'd been part of the family. His leaving was like a death, not only for her, but for everyone who had come to love him. She realized, as she watched the scene unfold, that she hadn't just been concerned about her own ability to love someone new, but also that of those she cared about.

After supper was finished, her momma brought out coffee and a tray of cannoli.

Julianne wiped the powdered sugar from her lips and rose to clear the table. "Amazing as always, Momma."

Her momma held out her hand to stop Julianne. "Let me get that. You go visit and play with the babies."

"Are you sure? I don't mind helping."

"Nonsense."

Jokob pushed back his chair, leaned over, and kissed her momma on the cheek. "Dinner was delicious. You've made me feel welcome here."

Julianne took Jokob's hand and followed Bella, Alex, and the little ones into the living room. Jokob plopped onto the floor and picked up a Lego piece. He held it out to Nicky. "Can you show me how this works?"

Nicky dropped his little bottom down on the floor in front of Jokob. "Ith eathie. I thow you," he said, with a slight lisp.

Nicky instructed Jokob on the intricacies of Lego's, building a small tower. Jokob played with this chatty three-year-old until Nicky moved onto trucks, apparently deciding they would be more exciting. Isabella joined in on the fun and used Jokob as her own personal climbing wall. Jokob rolled over onto his back and lifted her high into the air. Her squeal of delight rang throughout the house.

As Julianne watched Jokob play with the children, something inside reached an awareness she'd kept hidden from herself since Clay left. Her arms ached for a baby, a child of her own. Would Jokob consider children after his losses? *Whoa, girl. Going a little fast aren't you? You've only known each other a few weeks.*

twenty-three

*J*ulianne made morning rounds on day one of her four-day rotation, pushing the med-cart, when crying beckoned her to one of the rooms. She opened the door and found Edwina standing in her crib, soaked from head to toe. Julianne glanced around for a parent or other relative, but the room was empty, except for the child. It was odd for her to be alone. *They must be getting breakfast.*

Julianne pressed the call button. "I need an aid in 404. The baby and bed both need to be changed. And this is Spanish speaking only, so please send Anna."

She grabbed a towel from the bathroom and removed the child's clothes. The little girl pulled on Julianne to pick her up. "There, there. You'll be fine," she murmured in Spanish.

Once the clothes were off, she wrapped Edwina in the towel and scooped her up, careful of the IV tube and thigh-high cast. She carried her to the rocking chair, sat down with her, and began rocking and singing, "Hush little baby, don't you cry." *I'm going to need to learn some new songs when I have children.* It made her laugh at how funny and quaint she was to sing such an old song.

She stroked the little girl's hair, still singing and rocking. When Anna came in to change the bed, Julianne startled and blushed.

"She's such a sweetheart," Anna said, stripping off

the wet sheets. "Where is her mother?" Anna's accent was thick, having only arrived from San Salvador four years earlier.

The child settled and stopped crying, only moments before the door burst open and an older woman rushed in rapid firing questions in Spanish. Julianne asked her to speak a bit slower so she could understand, "Por favor más despacio."

The distraught woman took a breath and spoke slowly. "I am her Abuela. What happened? My daughter only left a few minutes ago. She had to go to work."

The little girl squirmed around in Julianne's lap at the sound of the woman and cried out, straining her arms toward the older woman.

Julianne stood and moved toward the child's grandmother. "She's alright, she's just wet and needs a bath. Would you like to bathe her or do you want the aid to do it?"

"Can I? I'm afraid of hurting her." The grandmother placed her belongings in the chair, came over, and picked up the toddler.

"It's not a problem. I'll have Anna show you." Julianne glanced at her buzzing pager and addressed the aid working on the bedding. "I need to take this page. Can you take this?"

Julianne placed her hand on the grandmother's arm. "Everything will be okay."

As she exited the child's room, Beverly ran toward her.

"Julianne, I paged you. You need to get to the ER next door stat! It's your dad!" Beverly's top-heavy chest heaved from running.

"What?"

"I don't know. They said for you to hurry."

Julianne handed the med-cart and her clipboard to her and raced for the stairwell. She hit the door at a full run, slamming it open. Its echo rang in her ears. After taking the stairs from the third to the first floor, she sprinted the three interior blocks through the twists and turns of the hospital to the ER. Slowing her gait, she flashed her badge over the keypad on the side security door to gain entry.

She darted to the nurse's bay and held out her badge, her breath coming in sucking gasps.

"Garvoli?"

"Bed four," the nurse replied, twisting in her chair to point behind her.

Julianne struggled to regain her composure and slow her ragged breath as she speed-walked to the other side of the large square room. Her momma waited outside the curtained room, tears streaming down her face.

"Momma, what happened?"

He momma grabbed her. "It's bad. I don't know if... oh Jules."

Julianne held onto her momma to keep her from collapsing.

"What, tell me?" Julianne looked up and did a double take seeing her poppy rushing toward her. She jerked her head to shake the image. No, it was George.

"What happened?" Her brother searched Julianne's face for answers.

"I don't know. Please, take Momma to the waiting room, and I'll find out." Julianne released her grip as George stepped close. With a deep inhale, she slipped through the curtain.

A scene she'd participated in many times—a tiny ER room crammed with equipment, doctors, and nurses, all moving in a well-orchestrated dance—swirled around her. Her poppy laid on the gurney, shirt open, bright red defibrillator marks on his chest, IV bag hanging to his right, and oxygen mask covering his mouth and nose.

Julianne placed her hand on her chest. "Poppy?" Her voice cracked as she tried to reach him, her way blocked by a doctor and a nurse, each busily playing their part in this life or death drama.

"Get her out of here!" one doctor barked, but stopped when he saw her. "Julianne?"

"That's my dad. What—"

"We've got this." Dr. Merk interrupted, gently touching her arm, latching his gaze onto hers. "Maybe you should wait outside. You know we're doing everything we can."

"Tell me, I need to know," Julianne pleaded through her tears.

"Your father had a massive heart attack. We've already had to revive him three times—once in the ambulance and twice here. His heart can't take much more."

Julianne's hand jerked to her mouth as she stifled a gasp.

"Help him," she choked, stepping out of the room, closing the curtain behind her.

Julianne joined her mother and brother, huddled together in the far corner of the waiting room. She pulled out her phone and dialed.

"Bella?" she managed to squeak out through the lump in her throat when voice mail picked up. "Poppy's at the Barnes ER. Come, quickly."

She hung up and dialed again.

"Jokob?" Her voice stretched to a tiny thread of sound. "My poppy. It's not good. I need you."

"Oh, no. What can I do?"

"Come to the ER at Barnes on Kingshighway?"

"I'm around the corner at the gallery. I'm on my way."

Julianne hung up the phone and took a seat, a sense of numb anxiety sinking into her belly. *This can't be happening.*

"Garvoli?" She looked up and took a deep breath.

All three rose and the charge nurse led them to his bedside. "He's stable for now. Please don't stay long. He needs his rest."

Julianne and her momma each held one of her poppy's hands and took turns kissing his forehead. George paced at the foot of the bed.

Her momma looked at her and George and said, "We should pray."

They bowed their heads and became silent.

The curtain rustled and Julianne peeked through slit eyes, seeing Jokob hanging back.

Her momma recited the Lord's Prayer. With "Amen," Julianne raised her tear-stained face and motioned for Jokob to join them. She held out her other hand to him, not wanting to release her poppy's.

Jokob came to her, wrapping her in his arms and kissing her cheek. "What happened?"

"He had a heart attack. He's already coded three times, I don't know how much more his heart can take."

"He's strong." Jokob looked over at her momma. "I'm here if there's anything you need."

"Thank you, Jokob. That's very kind."

The charge nurse came to the curtain. "He needs to rest. Mrs. Garvoli, you can stay if you'd like."

George left, followed by Julianne holding Jokob's hand. Her momma lingered behind for a few more minutes of private time with her husband.

Julianne woke with a start at the sound of the overhead speaker paging Dr. Merk, stat to ER bed four. Her heart leaped into her throat and she jumped out of her seat. Jokob grabbed her arm and restrained her from running.

"Jewel, let them do their job. They will come for you."

Julianne paced. The clock on the wall clicked by five, ten, fifteen minutes. When the charge nurse came around the corner toward them, Julianne stopped mid-stride.

"Please come with me."

Instead of taking them back to his bedside, the nurse ushered them toward a private family room. *No, not the room. Please God, not the room.*

Julianne caught the emptiness in Dr. Merk's expression, as he entered, and knew. She took her momma's right hand; George took the other.

He stopped in front of the three of them, head bowed. When he looked directly at them, defeat etched on his face. "I'm so very sorry, Mrs. Garvoli. The damage to your husband's heart was too great. We couldn't save him."

Her momma screamed, "No," and her legs buckled. Jokob caught her and eased her to the couch. George and Julianne wrapped themselves around her, sobs consuming the small room. Jokob hovered behind Julianne, a hand resting on her shoulder.

Dr. Merk touched Julianne's shoulder. When she looked up, he said, "I'm so sorry. You can see him when you're ready. Take your time."

He opened the door, running headlong into Bella.

Bella stopped dead in her tracks, taking in the mass of huddled loved ones in the room. "Oh God, no."

twenty-four

*J*ulianne huddled on the couch in her pajamas, covered in blankets, hugging a pillow. She alternated between shivering under the covers and throwing them off in a fit of heat. Her poppy's funeral had been yesterday, and her entire body ached with the rawness of her emotions.

She'd spent the first five days after his death with her momma. Last night, after the service, her momma had told her and George, "I need to be alone." Julianne had taken a week of bereavement leave from work but now was wondering if she'd actually feel better working.

All night she tossed and turned, but sleep evaded her. Yawning, she moved to the couch and dozed off and on to the sound of *Cinema Paradiso*, her poppy's favorite old Italian movie. The ring of her phone startled her awake, but she pulled her blanket over her head, not wanting to talk to anyone. She fluffed the pillows and drifted into a fitful sleep.

When it rang again, she glanced at the number. *Jokob.* A tiny hint of excitement filled her heart, and she answered.

"Jewel. How are you this morning?"

"Nothing feels real. I can't believe Poppy is gone. I miss him so much already."

"Is there anything I can do?"

"Not really. I'm going to stay curled up on the couch

today. I may go see Bella and the babies in the morning. Perhaps their laughter will help me feel better."

"I have a location I need to go to for a shoot. I didn't want to plan anything without checking with you."

"You should go, I'll be fine."

"You sure? I'll be gone overnight. I want to get a cabin at Meramec State Park so I can catch the sunrise. Their website says cell reception is spotty at best. You might not be able to reach me. But I wanted to check with you first, you're priority one."

"That's so sweet." Julianne blinked back tears, glad to feel something other than the gut wrenching pain of the past five days. She was grateful Jokob had been there, but cherished the space he gave her; she needed it.

"I should be done and back around two tomorrow afternoon. Would you like me to come over after that? We can simply sit on the couch together if you'd like."

"I think I'd like that."

"'K, I'll call you when I'm close."

"Bye."

Ben and Jerry climbed all over her, seeking attention and begging for sustenance. Julianne shuffled to the kitchen. She poured dry food into their bowls, adding some canned as a special treat. Both cats wove in and out of her legs and stretched their feet up on her thigh at the whir of the can opener. Their meows filled the small space.

She slid out the coffee maker and inserted a pod. *Coffee might perk me up.* While it was brewing, she pulled down a bowl and a box of cereal. She ate at the island, attempting to read the newspaper. After re-reading the same story three times, she gave up and headed back to the couch.

She clicked on the TV and scanned. *How can I possibly have 500 stations and nothing to watch?* She finally settled on a channel with back-to-back, alternating *Jerry Seinfeld* and *Friends* reruns.

Around three, she called Mangiano's Pizza and ordered her favorite meat lover's deep-dish pizza.

Stuffed from pizza, and in spite of dozing off and on all day, she dragged herself to bed after the evening news. As she drifted to sleep, all she could think about was the futility of life. No matter what she did, she would die. Everyone would die.

A loud whack from nearby lightning shook her from a sound sleep a few hours later. A quick check of her weather app confirmed the threat of thunderstorms all day, with a high risk of flash flooding. *Forecasters got it wrong again. Ah well, I'm safe on the second floor, good sleeping weather.* She inserted earplugs and quickly drifted back to sleep.

She awoke about seven and decided she would definitely head over to Bella's after breakfast for a morning with the bambinos. *They certainly won't be going anywhere in this weather.*

"Auntie Jules!" Nicky screamed, as he and Isabella tackled Julianne at the door.

"I am so glad you braved this storm. The kids are already nuts from being trapped inside." Bella wrapped her arms

205

around her friend. "How are you doing?" Bella kissed Julianne on both cheeks. "I still can't believe he's gone."

"I'm ok today. I finally got a good night's sleep. A morning with the kids will be good for me." Julianne loved nothing more than spoiling her adopted niece and nephew rotten, leaving Bella with the mess.

They'd barely begun playing with a wild mixture of trucks and dolls when the howl of a tornado siren began far in the distance, escalating to a crescendo. Julianne's tornado app also shrieked its warning. Nicky's wail grew to match both. He raced to his room and slid under his bed.

"Nicky?" Julianne ran behind him and caught his foot before it disappeared into the darkness. "Come out, Nicky. We need to get to the base—" A crack of lightning struck close enough to cause the hair on her arms to stand out. A deep rumble of thunder followed and the wood-frame house trembled with its roar.

She tugged on Nicky's foot, dragging him out. She grabbed his hand and shouted, "Come on, sweetie. We've got to go."

Nicky wiggled out of Julianne's arms and sprinted to the basement door, down the steps and into the walled-off shelter. Alex had built it last spring after a tornado shredded his best friend's house, killing his wife.

Balancing Isabella on one hip and Peanut on the other, Bella followed Nicky and Julianne to the shelter. Julianne checked the storm's path on the 5-inch TV Alex kept in the room.

"Wow," she said under her breath. "It's really close." She checked Meramec—light rain, relieved for Jokob, but growing more frightened for them.

Nicky climbed into her lap, trembling. "Make ith stop."

"We're okay, little buddy. It's just a big rain." She did her best to sound calm for him, but her heart raced remembering the last tornado that hit the area. The Good Friday tornadoes, the news had called it. Easter would never be the same for the people whose homes were flattened, reduced to kindling.

She smoothed Nicky's hair, thinking about some of the youngest victims that had come to her hospital. A lump rose in her throat when one scene flashed through her mind—a limp two-year-old died in her arms after being tossed hundreds of feet through the air, landing in a tree.

The sound of those sirens, once ignored as being silly, now commanded great respect.

They huddled in the basement, listening to the shriek of the wind whipping around the corners of the house. Nicky jerked, when something hit and shattered a window upstairs. He wailed in harmony with the wind that threatened to blow the house down. Julianne wrapped one hand around a two-by-four wall post, the other arm around Nicky.

Julianne held him close. "It's okay, *Tesoro*, we're safe down here." She hoped she was convincing, as the child snuggled in close with his head on Julianne's chest. He sucked his thumb in rhythm with her racing heart. Julianne placed a hand over the child's other ear.

As quickly as it began, the storm was over, as if someone had flicked a switch. A check of the local broadcast revealed how close they'd come to being on the news themselves—less than a quarter of a mile away, multiple houses were shredded. No injuries had been reported.

When she released a sigh, Julianne realized she'd been holding her breath.

Julianne carried Nicky upstairs and to a window to assure him they were safe. "See, everything's good."

He clung to her, arms wrapped around her neck and waist. Julianne rubbed his back as she followed Bella to survey the broken window. It was in the main floor bathroom, and other than glass, there was no damage. Bella called Alex to tell him they were safe and let him know about the window.

After hanging up, they took the kids back to the living room, hoping to distract them from what had happened. It worked. Within minutes, they were playing, the danger forgotten.

Bella asked, "So we didn't get a chance to talk before everything happened with Poppy. What's going on with Jokob?"

"We've decided to give it a shot. I've spent too much of my life playing it safe." Julianne beamed.

Bella jumped up and down, clapping her hands in delight, something little myna bird Isabella tried to mimic. At fourteen months, she was doing and saying everything she saw and heard.

"He's coming over later today. We're going to hang out on the couch. He stayed overnight at Meramec State Park."

Julianne swept Isabella up and swung her around the room. "Weee!" they both squealed.

"Wow, in this storm? I hope his goal was to take pictures of rain drops."

"Ha! Good one! There was absolutely nothing about a storm forecasted on the news yesterday. The weather app shows only spotty showers out that way, he should be good."

Julianne checked her watch—close to one o'clock.

She laid a hand on Bella's shoulder. "You good here?"

"I think so now. Alex will be home any minute to board up the window."

"Okay, then I'm gonna go so I'll be home when Jokob calls. Thanks so much for the 'fun,'" she emphasized with air quotes. "Always an adventure. Love you."

Julianne gave a flourish of hugs and kisses all around and headed home.

Bella answered her phone on the fourth ring. "Hang on… I'm wrestling a wiggling butt into a diaper," she shouted into the speakerphone. "Phew. I can't figure out how all that smell comes out of this tiny human. I thought you had a date."

"I did too. It's almost three and Jokob hasn't called. I've tried calling his cell several times, but it goes straight to voicemail. He said he'd be back by two."

"Wait, where'd you say he was going?" The tone in Bella's voice clicked up an octave.

"Meramec State Park."

"Oh crap, I just heard on the news that the camp got hit by a tornado and flash floods about three hours ago, when we were in the basement. They're evacuating everyone."

The hair on the back of Julianne's neck stood on end. She hung up and dropped her phone.

She ran to her bedroom, changed back to jeans from her pajama pants, and pulled on hiking boots. Not bothering to tuck in her hot pink t-shirt, she grabbed her phone and raced out the door. It was almost an hour and a half drive, even without rain. She had no plan, other than she had to get there and fast.

twenty-five

Traffic was sparse due to the viciousness of the storm, which continued to pelt the area. Julianne passed multiple accidents and cars idled on the shoulder. She scanned for Jokob's red Jeep heading the other direction or in the median. Two hours later, she reached a scene of pure chaos at the camp entrance. The closed gate stretched across the road, with emergency vehicles and rescue crews everywhere. She pulled up to a police officer directing traffic out of the park.

"I have to get in," she yelled through pounding rain, punctuated by flashes of lightning and thunder.

"No one's allowed in," he shouted through a wall of rain. "We're still trying to rescue trapped campers. You can park over there and wait." He motioned to an area away from the ambulances.

Panicked, Julianne parked, and jumped out of her car into ankle deep mud and water. She glanced over at the nearest ambulance. Soaked rescuers loaded a gurney into it. On the ground, surrounded by flowing mud, lay a row of filled body bags. She gasped. Her heart leaped into her throat, and she ran toward the bags, but another officer stood in her way. She got close enough to know by the size of the bodies in the bags, that none of them was large enough to be Jokob. Her heart broke—*children*.

She slogged up the road that led into the campgrounds, her clothes already soaked. Sheets of rain pelted her eyes making it hard to see past twenty feet ahead.

The guard posted at the gate stopped her. "You can't go in. Too dangerous!" he yelled over the storm's howl.

"I've got to get in there," she screamed, struggling to run past him.

He outsized her and held tight to her arm. She threw up her free hand in surrender and relaxed her body. The guard loosened his grip, and when he did, Julianne wiggled her wrist free and ran. The guard followed but slid in the mud and fell to his hands and knees. Julianne continued slipping and sliding in the mud sloughed gravel toward the campground and the river. The swollen river roared in the distance.

As she rounded the bend, the impact of destruction became evident. Campers lay on their sides and upside down, some caught in tree roots in the river. Cabins were simply gone, only their concrete bases remained. The sight stopped Julianne in her tracks, unable to comprehend this level of destruction.

"Jokob!" she screamed repeatedly into the wind and rain, while turning in slow, slippery circles.

"Jewel, look out!"

Jokob gestured wildly at something behind her. She turned in time to see a wall of muddy water rushing toward her as the last levee breached. The mud wall slammed full force into her chest, cutting off her scream and sucking her under, propelling her full-tilt down river.

Jokob ran alongside the bank, desperate to stay in view of Julianne's bobbing head and flailing arms. The raging river carried her away faster than he could run in the mud that sucked on his boots with each step. In the distance, her hot-pink t-shirt stopped, her limp body caught in the roots of a tree growing from the bank. Using the shoulder-communicator, provided when he volunteered to help with the rescue mission, he radioed for help before slogging toward the pink blur.

The swirl of the river swept Julianne off its main destructive path and into an inner eddy where tree roots held her tight. Jokob tied one end of his rescue team rope around a tree higher up on the bank and the other end around his waist. He waded toward her, fighting the current threatening to yank him under. As he reached her, the rescue team arrived. He placed a harness around her lifeless body as gently as possible and signaled the team to pull them both to safety.

"She's unconscious and not breathing," Jokob yelled over the river's roar to the rescue team.

Mack, the team lead started water rescue CPR while Jokob paced. Julianne's complexion was already a sickening shade of blue-gray. Tears streamed down Jokob's face and mixed with the rain. He paced behind the team, muttering under his breath. *What was she doing out here? Please, you have to wake up.*

A small cough, followed by a larger one, combined with a rush of water and escaped Julianne's lips.

"She's breathing!" Mack yelled. "Get her on the board. Careful of her spine."

The team slipped and fought their way up the muddy hill to an awaiting ambulance. Jokob followed close behind.

"You know this woman?" Mack asked Jokob.

"She's my girlfriend. I didn't know she was out here."

"Hop on in, son. You're done here," Mack said, patting Jokob on the shoulder.

Jokob placed a foot on the ambulance step and hesitated, feeling the world swirl ever so slightly. He shook his head and climbed in after the stretcher, careful to stay clear of the EMTs while they worked.

"Julianne, wakeup. Please," he whispered to her. He waited a breath before a scream ripped from his lips. "Wake up."

Her eyelids fluttered open. The ambulance siren wailed and they headed out of the park. She drifted in and out of consciousness, Jokob holding her hand the whole time.

What should have been a fifteen-minute drive to the hospital in Sullivan took close to an hour, due to flooding and storm debris that littered the road. Jokob focused on Julianne to shut out the whirring in his head from the memory of his last ambulance ride.

The ER staff raced out the door, when they arrived, rushing Julianne into an open bay. They directed Jokob to wait in the lounge.

"I'm not leaving her," he said calmly but firmly. He'd learned many things during Keara's illness, and one was that if you remain calm, they let you stay.

On the inside, he was anything but calm. He gripped his hands into fists, the nails digging into this palms. He seethed with anger at Julianne for putting herself in such danger. *What the hell was she doing there in the middle of a storm anyway? Did she drive through that storm for*

214

me? Jokob stepped back to let a nurse pass. *Would I have done the same for her?* Rubbing his hand over his beard, he huffed. He couldn't lose her, not now, not ever. Any doubts he might have had before about his feelings for her were washed away by that river.

He hovered in the background while the ER team moved her from the gurney to the bed and took vital signs. Shifting from one foot to another, the noise threatened dark places in his mind.

The staff worked with practiced speed, each having a role to play and playing it without a hitch. When they wheeled Julianne off for x-rays and a head CT, Jokob paced in the family area. An ambulance pulled into the bay with no siren, no lights. He peered around the corner. The crew pulled out a sheet-draped gurney. The victim was obviously pregnant. Bile rose in his throat.

Minutes stretched to hours before the doctor came to the door. "Garvoli?"

Jokob jumped and ran over. "How bad is she?"

"And you are?" the doctor questioned.

"Her husband," Jokob lied. He'd obtain more information that way; they would never ask for proof.

"It's too soon to say for sure, but she's suffered some level of head trauma. She's been in and out of consciousness since she arrived." The doctor spoke with the determined manner of an ER doctor with many years under his belt.

Jokob relaxed a bit, sensing this doctor knew his stuff. But it was short-lived as the walls seemed to tighten around him. He sucked in a big breath and released it in a rush.

"We won't know for sure the degree of head injury until she wakes up completely. We're moving her to ICU where we'll wait while her brain heals. She also has three cracked ribs and a severely bruised sternum, possibly from the CPR, contusions on her back and neck, but no internal organ damage. Some deep lacerations and major bruises. And we'll need to watch her for aspiration pneumonia. With all that, I'm truly surprised she suffered no other broken bones given all the breaks we've seen, at least in the patients coming in alive."

The doctor put his hand on Jokob's arm. "Look, it may be a while, days even, before we know anything definitive. You should go home and get some rest. Come back tomorrow."

Jokob shook his head. "I'll stay. I could use some dry clothes though. Could I get a set of scrubs?"

"Sure." The doctor signaled an orderly over, requested the scrubs, and moved on to his next patient. Fortunately, the initial crush of incoming patients from the storm had slowed, but there were still many to be seen.

Jokob slipped into the men's room and changed into the scrubs, using an ER bag for his wet things. His cell phone dripped. *Not working tonight.* Leaning over, he put his head in his hands and closed his eyes. *I can do this.*

Poking his head into Julianne's area in the ICU, he decided it was safe to grab a quick bite. He hadn't eaten since breakfast and it was long past dark. He stopped at the nurse's station.

"Could someone call her mother? My phone is soaked from the storm and I'm sure Julianne's was lost. Her mother is Sibeal Garvoli. It might be listed under

Giorgio Garvoli. She lives in The Hill neighborhood in St. Louis."

"Thank you. We'll find her." The charge nurse patted his arm in the way a mother might soothe a baby. "She'll be fine. Go get some food and rest a bit. There are couches in the waiting area. We'll fill you in when you return. And we can always page you on the intercom if anything changes."

Reluctantly, Jokob did as she advised and headed to the cafeteria. The food smelled good, but lay like a ball of lead in his stomach. He pushed it from side to side on the plate, finally giving up and tossing most of it in the trash.

On the way back to Julianne's room, he passed the chapel and stopped, lingering outside the doors. He hadn't been in a church since before Keara's death—*what good had his prayers done then?* He went in anyway.

An elderly man, with thinning white hair and bowed head, occupied the first pew. At the creak of the door, the man lifted his head and nodded in Jokob's direction. He had the look of a kindly grandfather.

Jokob ran his hand along the top of the back pew, before slinking into the seat. He bowed his head. He was startled when the elderly man appeared beside him.

"You look like you could use some help with whatever's troubling you, son. Do you mind if I sit with you?"

"Not at all." Jokob gestured to the seat.

"What brings you to the chapel this stormy night, son?" The elderly man had gentle eyes, the sort that showed wisdom gained from decades of living.

"My girlfriend… got caught in that storm. She's pretty messed up." Tears stung Jokob's eyes to talk about it.

"May I pray with you?"

The calming presence of the elderly gentleman helped Jokob feel lighter. "Thank you so much. I appreciate the support. I hadn't thought to find myself in a hospital tonight, much less a chapel." Realizing he had no idea why this man was here, he asked, "May I ask why you're in the chapel?"

"My beloved Margaret died in the storm when a tree fell on our house. I came in here to help with her journey to the other side." Now those old eyes shone with tears and grief.

Jokob inhaled sharply and took the old man's hands in his. "I'm so sorry for your loss."

"Thank you, son. She was eighty-seven. Married seventy years we were. This was better than the alternative. You see, Margaret had late-stage Alzheimer's. She no longer remembered me, or our children, grandchildren, or great-grandchildren. Everything frightened her, and she required sedation much of the time. So, this was better. Faster. Cleaner. She can go be at peace now." He had transformed while speaking and now shone with joy and a bright smile.

"Son, thank you for allowing me to pray with you." His gnarled, liver-spotted hand patted Jokob's knee. "Margaret would have liked you." He rose on shaking legs and scuffled out.

Jokob sat stunned after the man left, eternally grateful he had been there.

twenty-six

*J*okob rounded the last corner before the nurse's station and saw Mrs. Garvoli talking with the doctor. He quickened his pace. When he placed his hand on her shoulder, she startled.

"Jokob what happened?" Her voice quivered. She burst into tears and reached for the safety of his arms.

Jokob patted her back, and faced toward the doctor. "Has there been any change?"

"No. As we discussed, and I was explaining to Mrs. Garvoli, we won't know the extent of the brain injury until she wakes up."

"Brain injury?" Mrs. Garvoli's hand flew to her mouth, her eyes begging the doctor.

"Mrs. Garvoli, your daughter has a concussion and she's been in and out of consciousness. We need to give her brain a chance to heal. Once she wakes up, we'll know more, and learn whether there's any permanent damage."

The doctor gave Mrs. Garvoli a quick rundown of Julianne's other injuries, but it seemed all she heard was brain damage.

When the doctor was finished, Jokob led her to the waiting area where she slumped into a chair. Jokob took her hand. "Mrs. Garvoli, I know we've barely met and not under ideal circumstances—"

"Please call me Sibeal," she interrupted.

"Sibeal, I'm in love with your daughter. I didn't know for sure until I saw that wall of water hit her. You should know... I told the staff I'm her husband. I figured they'd never let me stay, and certainly wouldn't talk to me, if I told them the truth."

"It's all right. I understand and am glad you told me so I don't mess it up."

Her face drawn taut held eyes liquid with fear.

"Bella called me, hysterical. She said Jules hung up on her when she heard about the tornado. I tried to reach her several times, frantic with worry, before the hospital called." She twisted in her chair. "My God, Jokob, what happened? Why was she out there in a storm? It's not like her at all."

Jokob hung his head. "I think she was there to save me."

"Save you?" Sibeal furrowed her brow.

"She knew I'd gone out to Meramec for an overnight so I could shoot pictures of the sunrise. I guess when she heard about the tornado strike out there, she panicked. She probably tried to call me, but there was no service. The rescue team conscripted me to help with the rescue effort, and I was working on clearing out campers when I heard someone screaming my name. That's when I saw the wall of mud racing toward her."

Sibeal shook her head, covering her mouth with her hand.

"Sibeal, I'm so sorry. She shouldn't have been there." Jokob laid his head back on the seat and shut his eyes.

They sat, silently lost in their own thoughts. Finally, Sibeal spoke.

"Did you know Jules was a preemie? She was born almost two months early and spent her first few weeks fighting for her life. We almost lost her a couple of times. First, to pneumonia. Later, she got one of those hospital staph infections…I forget which one. She's tough and no matter what, I have faith she'll pull through this and come out even stronger."

Jokob pondered Sibeal's words hoping she was right. "I'm going to stay out here until she's out of danger. I think I'll get a room at the hotel so I can shower and maybe get some sleep. How 'bout you?"

"I really haven't thought about it. The hospital called and I raced out here. I didn't bring any clothes or medications, or anything."

Jokob bolted straight up. "Cooper. I need to get my dog and find some place to board him. I wonder if the hotel allows dogs. If not, I'll have to find a kennel. I can leave him one, maybe two, nights on his own, but I don't know how long I'll be here."

"Why don't you go." It was more a statement than a question. "I'll stay until you return. I'll go home for clothes and things after that. I need to find someone to keep my fur-baby, Angel."

"I hate to, but… " As much as Jokob wanted to stay, he needed to get away. He'd managed a few hours in the hospital, but the walls pressed in closer around him, threatening to suck him into a deep pit.

"I won't be long. My RV is a few miles past Six Flags on Highway 44." Jokob stood to leave, but stopped and looked back. "I know you don't know me, but I doubt if I'll be at the hotel much. We could share a room and alternate shifts if you'd like. I can get a spare key when I check in."

Sibeal looked up at the man her daughter had chosen to date. "I guess if Jules trusts you, I can too. That would be good."

twenty-seven

Day 4

Sibeal arrived in Julianne's room shortly after eight a.m., and tried not to wake Jokob, but he woke anyway. Sheer exhaustion had finally forced her to get a good night's sleep in the hotel.

Dr. Mallory arrived at nine, as promised, and ran through Julianne's vitals check.

"The nurses told me she's been drifting in and out of consciousness. Has she said anything to you?" Dr. Mallory asked, shining his pen light into Julianne's eyes.

"Just gibberish. Nothing that made any sense." Sibeal pressed her fist into her lips.

"That is completely normal. It could still be days before she is fully awake. We simply don't know."

"Isn't there something that can be done to wake her?"

"Mrs. Garvoli, as I explained before, there isn't. In fact, sleep is the best thing possible to allow her to heal. The brain is complex and difficult to predict."

Sibeal and Jokob took turns going for breakfast and coffee so one of them could be with her at all times. Back in the room, Jokob nodded off in the chair.

Sibeal shook him by the shoulder. "You should go get some rest. I'll call you if anything changes."

"No, I want to be here when she wakes," he protested, stifling a yawn.

"I realize I'm not your mother, but I *am* Julianne's. You won't do her any good if you don't get some sleep. I insist. Now, go." Sibeal stretched all five-foot three inches of her stature up straight, head up, shoulders back. Placing her hands on her hips, she gave Jokob her best do-as-I-say stare.

"Ok, you win. I really am beat." He kissed Julianne on the forehead. He headed for the door, stopping short. "Promise you'll call?"

Day 6

Julianne woke screaming and swearing at the nurse trying to take her blood pressure. Shocked at the words spewing from her daughter, Sibeal said, "Dear Lord," and put her hand over her mouth, apologizing to the nurse. "I am so sorry. I didn't even know she knew words like those."

"Honey, it's perfectly alright. In fact, it's better, it's wonderful. The brain can do weird things when it's healing. The fact she's talking means her speech center is waking up. Maybe the rest of her will soon as well."

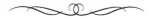

Day 8

Julianne's eyes flicked open. She hard-blinked, fighting to see through the grease-like film that seemed to block her vision. She willed herself to wake, unable to tell if she was awake or in one of those dreams where you try to wake up but can't. She'd been trying for days.

She struggled to understand her surroundings: curtains closed, room dark, incessant beeping—*what is that sound? Wait, I should know. What is it? Wait, I know what that is. But… why?* She tried to sit up and cried out in pain.

"Jewel?" A man leaped to her side. He flipped on the bedside light and grabbed the call button.

"She's awake again," he said, reaching out to touch her face.

Julianne flinched at his touch. She fought to focus, the images in the room moving in and out of sharp and blurred definition. When she could finally make out a face, she found herself staring into the most intense crystal-green eyes.

"Where?" The insides of her mouth scraped like sandpaper.

"Water." She managed to squeak out.

The man dipped a small sponge-on-a-stick into a cup of water and squeezed the excess. He held it to her lips. "You're in the hospital."

Her eyes tracked his every move. *Why is there a man in my room in the middle of the night? Wait, did he just call me Jewel?* She lifted her right hand and stared at the pulse oximeter attached to her index finger and IV coming out of the back of her hand. She groaned.

"What?" As the walls of the room waved and swooped from side-to-side, her vision threatened to slither out of focus again.

"Do you remember anything? Do you know why you're here?"

Julianne shook her head and the spinning intensified. She took a deep breath to try to stabilize. Her brow creased in deep concentration. "Who are," she paused, each word a struggle. "Who, are you?"

The man stopped cold. "I'm Jokob."

"Jokob?" she pondered, the crease in her forehead deepened. "Do I know you? Did you call me Jewel? Why?"

"The doctor said you might have memory issues at first." He flipped on the overhead.

Julianne blanched from the light, but she saw him better.

"Take your time. I called you Jewel because that's what I call you." He moved back to the side of the bed and took her hand. "We're dating."

Julianne jerked her hand away and shook her head again, slowly this time so she could control the room. She stared hard, but her brain felt like pea soup—murky and full of lumps.

"Something about you seems familiar, sort of like from a dream—all fuzzy and altered. Is my momma here? Poppy?"

"Your mom's asleep at the hotel. I'll call her."

Sibeal threw on clothes and ran a brush through her hair, grabbed her purse, and headed for the hospital. Her heart and head raced. *What will I find when I get there?*

She stopped outside Julianne's door to take a few calming, deep breaths before stepping inside. The room was dark, and Jokob met her at the door guiding her back into the hallway.

"She's out again," he whispered, laying his hand on her arm. "But she was awake and talking, so things aren't as bad as feared. But she does have some memory loss." Looking at his shoes, he added, "She doesn't know me. And she asked for Giorgio."

226

Sibeal took a sharp intake of breath and held it before allowing the air to seep from her lips, like a slowly leaking balloon. She leaned on the wall for support as she worked to gain control of her emotions.

"Oh dear. She doesn't know her poppy is gone, and she doesn't know you. So she's lost, what a month? More?" Her voice quaked with trepidation.

"We don't know yet. The doctor hasn't been in, but I don't really expect him until morning."

"Why don't you go get some rest? I'll stay with her. I need to be here when she wakes up again. She needs me."

Jokob knew Sibeal was right, but inside he was screaming. *This can't be happening.* He stepped back into the room and grabbed his backpack. He looked over at Julianne, turned his head toward Sibeal, and slipped back out the door.

"Momma?"

Sibeal roused with a start and almost tripped getting to the bedside. "I'm here, sweetie. What do you need?" She firmly planted a kiss on Julianne's forehead.

"Is Poppy here?" Julianne's gaze traced the room.

"Not right now." Sibeal struggled over when to tell her. "What's the last thing you remember?"

"I don't know, everything feels surreal, all broken up into tiny fragments. I can't tell what's real and what's a dream."

"It's alright, the doctor said your brain would be like scrambled eggs with pieces of broken shell for a little while. You took a hard blow to your head."

227

"What happened? How did I end up here? And where exactly is... here?"

"You're in the hospital in Sullivan. You almost drowned in a flood at Meramec State Park. Jokob saved you."

"Jokob?" Julianne frowned, a flit of recognition darted across her face. "That man that was here before, right?"

"That's right."

"Who is he? He said we're dating, but, Momma, I don't know him. I think it hurt him that I didn't remember."

Sibeal pulled her chair closer to the bed. She picked up Julianne's hand and bowed her head in prayer. When she opened her eyes, tears had filled Julianne's, the moisture intensifying the denim-blue. She gazed lovingly at Julianne. "You met him about six weeks ago, and yes, you're dating. He's a very sweet man and has been here for you. I've practically had to force him to go get rest and food."

A light tap and the door to the room swung open. Dr. Mallory came in. "Good morning, Ms. Garvoli. It's good to see you awake. How are you feeling?"

"Like I've been clubbed over the head, dragged by a bus, and chewed on by wild dogs."

"Well, little lady, in a manner of speaking, you were. You're very lucky. It may not feel like it, but things could have been so much worse." Dr. Mallory shone his light into Julianne's eyes and casually checked vitals.

"I'm having trouble remembering things. People. Will I get that back?"

"Feels different on the other side doesn't it?" Dr. Mallory asked.

"Exactly! I know all of this, but now it doesn't make any sense. I feel like my brain is full of mashed potatoes."

"Short-term memory loss is common in head injuries and traumatic situations. It's one way our body copes with what it's undergoing. Sort of a protective mechanism. And trust me, young lady, you really don't want to regain the memory of what happened."

"Maybe not, but I'd like to at least remember that I'm dating this guy who's been hanging around here."

"What's the last thing you remember before the accident?"

Julianne furrowed her brow and looked side-to-side with her eyes, like she was trying to find something in her memory. "Maybe dinner with Bella? I'll think more about it later. Right now, I'm tired and my head hurts."

"I'll send in something for pain. Rest is the best thing for you right now. Tomorrow we're transferring you to Missouri Baptist in St. Louis. They are better equipped to aid in your further recovery. Plus, it will be much closer for your mother." Dr. Mallory paused, his arms crossed over his chest. "Do you have any questions?"

Julianne looked at the doctor, fear emblazoned in her eyes. "Did… did I die?"

Sibeal inhaled sharply.

"Why do you ask?" Dr. Mallory's calm demeanor remained unchanged.

"I remember being very cold and frightened one minute, and the next I was warm, in no pain with no fear. It was like I'd been wrapped in a warm blanket of love. And it was bright, blindingly bright. Someone screamed at me to wake up, and I was cold and in intense pain again."

Dr. Mallory placed his hand on Julianne's arm. "You coded three times in the ambulance."

229

twenty-eight

The ambulance arrived at Missouri Baptist Hospital around two p.m., followed by Jokob and her momma in their own cars.

The nurse hustled around getting Julianne settled in and taking her vitals.

"This all feels so strange, being on this side," Julianne said to the nurse attaching her blood pressure cuff and pulse ox.

"What do you mean?"

"I'm an RN at Children's. I've never been the patient before."

"Well, don't worry. We have excellent staff here who'll take good care of you." The nurse completed her tasks and started to leave, but stopped and turned back. "If there's anything you need, you know the drill."

"Thank you."

On her way out, the nurse held the door so Jokob and her momma could go in.

"Something's wrong," Julianne said, as her momma approached the bed. "What aren't you telling me?"

"What do you mean, sweetie?"

"Poppy hasn't been to see me. I'm scared. He'd never stay away."

Her momma glanced at Jokob and they exchanged an almost imperceptible nod.

"I'll be in the waiting area," Jokob said, and slipped out the door.

Her momma perched on the edge of the bed. She took Julianne's hand.

"There are so many things from the past few weeks you don't remember. I was hoping you would remember this, so you wouldn't have to go through it all again. The doctors say you're strong enough now." Her momma paused and looked at the ceiling through the tops of her eyes, trying to block the tears. "My sweet Jules," her voice cracked, "Your poppy suffered a massive heart attack two weeks ago. I'm so sorry, sweetie. He's gone."

Julianne doubled over, like she'd been punched in the gut. "No," she screamed. "Oh God, no." The wail that emanated from her sounded like a wounded animal.

Her momma wrapped her arms around her and rocked her until she sobbed herself to sleep.

Julianne awoke a few hours later to a semi-dark room. Bella's outline was curled up in the chair, her head resting on her rolled up purse.

"Bella?"

Bella woke and moved closer, taking Julianne's hand.

"Poppy died."

"I know, girlfriend. I'm so sorry. Sorry that he's gone, sorry that you didn't remember it and have to go through this again."

"How's Momma doing? First Poppy and now me all banged up, I'm worried about her."

"She's good, Jokob's been a huge help. They shared a hotel room while you were in Sullivan so Momma didn't have to drive back and forth. And Jokob's staying at her place now."

"Really? It's so odd that you all seem to know him, yet I don't. The last thing I remember is having dinner with you before some kind of… art show?" She pinched her eyes narrow, as if trying to peer into the past. "I remember telling you that I might go on a mission. Then nothing… like it happened a few minutes ago and we're heading to wherever we were heading. Did that really happen or is it a fragment from my scrambled brains?"

"It happened. You met Jokob at the art show. It was his show, he's a photographer.

Julianne slowly shook her head and released a thick sigh. "He seems nice, and is devilishly handsome, but I'm uncomfortable having him here. He so desperately wants me to remember him and," she paused, big tears rimming her lashes as she glanced at Bella, "I just… don't. I think I need him to stop coming here, at least for now. Until I find my bearings and start remembering again."

"What if you don't? Remember, I mean? I'm pretty sure he's in love with you and you told me the day of the accident you thought you were in love with him. Are you just gonna let that go?"

"How can I let go of something I don't even remember?" Julianne responded, frustration tingeing her voice. "I can't deal with that right now. I need to get better and it's too distracting having to worry about his feelings."

Jokob tapped lightly on Julianne's hospital door. "Jewel?" He poked his head in. "Ah, good, you're awake."

"Don't call me that." The razor sharp edge in Julianne's voice stopped Jokob in his tracks halfway through the door.

"Please, come in. We need to talk."

Jokob closed the door behind him and pulled up a chair. *This can't be good.*

Julianne drew a deep slow breath and released it, as if she was meditating. "I want to say thank you for saving my life."

Jokob moved toward her, but she held up her hand to stop him.

"Like I said, I appreciate what you did for me. But I can't do this whole guy-girl thing right now. I know people say we're dating. Bella says I told her I'm in love with you. But I don't remember any of that. I can't be worried about not knowing you or not having feelings for you while I'm trying to get my life, my brain back together."

"Julianne, please don't do this." Head down, Jokob struggled to keep from breaking.

"If you truly care for me, you'll do what I need. And right now, I need you to leave."

Jokob looked up, his face warped with despair, wet from tears. He opened and closed his mouth. Nothing he said would change anything. So he said nothing, picked up his bag and walked out.

Julianne huddled in the bed sobbing, but she couldn't remember why.

twenty-nine

*J*okob staggered down the hospital corridor toward the elevator, wiping his tears on his sleeve. He stopped at the entrance to the stairwell, his hand on the knob, seemingly frozen in place. In a burst, he twisted the door handle and shoved, dragged himself through, and shut the door.

Dropping his bag, he leaned his back against the wall. He slowly slid to the floor, small gasps escaping his lips. He tried sucking in air, but felt like he was drowning—none reached his lungs. He moaned and the sobs came forth in a rush that left him on the verge of collapse.

The door opened and a young doctor stepped into the stairwell, almost tripping over Jokob's legs. "Hey, you okay?"

Jokob ignored him and attempted to pull himself to legs that felt like jelly. He wobbled.

"Let me help you. Is there someone I can call?" The doctor reached for Jokob's arm to help him upright.

Jokob jerked away. "No one." The only person who could help had sent him away. "I'll be fine," he said, waving his hand. He dried his face on his shirt and staggered down the stairs.

On the ground floor, he exited and inhaled a big gulp of air. He found his Jeep and cranked the engine. For once, it purred and leaped to a start on the first try.

In a daze, he drove to Sibeal's house and used the key she'd given him. Cooper's anxious woof vibrated the door as Jokob clicked the lock.

"Jokob?" Sibeal said, running her hand over her hair. "You're back early. I wasn't expecting you for a few hours."

He looked toward but through her.

"Is everything alright? Is it Julianne?" She rose from the lounger and moved toward him.

Jokob shook his head and held up his hand. Sibeal stopped.

"She's fine. I… can't stay… have to go." He stumbled through the words and into the guestroom to gather his things.

Sibeal followed him. "I don't understand. Where do you need to go? Why?"

He didn't answer, simply stuffed all the items he'd brought in a few hours earlier back into his bag. He looked back and said, "Thank you, you've been more than kind." He hugged her, holding her tightly, lingering.

Turning around at the front door to look at the room one last time, he slapped his leg and called, "Cooper, come on buddy. Let's go for a ride." Cooper bounded in from the other room and raced out the door. He jumped over the half door of the Jeep into the front seat. Jokob circled to the other side, got in, and cranked the engine. He didn't look back.

Sibeal lingered in her doorway, as the Jeep disappeared, slowly shaking her head. She gathered her purse and returned to the hospital.

Jokob steered his Jeep west to Eureka, to his RV. He didn't notice other cars on the road, driving on autopilot.

He reached the campground around two o'clock. Cooper bounded out of the Jeep, chasing a squirrel up a tree. As soon as the RV door closed behind him, Jokob's throat tightened. He again felt like he couldn't breathe. The room spun and he slammed to the floor.

When he came to, he wasn't sure exactly where he was or how he'd gotten there. He rolled over and lifted himself to his knees, rubbing a large welt on the side of his head. *How did I get that?* Jokob recalled Julianne telling him to leave. He pulled himself up using the counter as leverage and glanced at the clock—four o'clock. *Damn, I was out a long time.*

Pulling his cell phone out, he dialed. "Deserai, it's Jokob. Look would it be too much of an inconvenience for you to ship my exhibit and payment on to Seattle without me?"

The sound of Deserai rubbing his beard reverberated in Jokob's ear. "Not at all, my friend. Is everything okay?"

"It's all good, but I want to head to Seattle a bit early. I'll text you the address."

"Of course. And, do please let me know when you will have a new exhibit. This one was well-received. I would love to have you back any time."

"Thank you. Later."

He stared at his phone and sighed heavily before texting, "Hey Kev... Call when you can."

Feeling bad about how he'd left Sibeal, he sent another text. "Sibeal, sorry I left the way I did. Julianne

237

asked me to leave and I can't stand the idea of sitting around waiting for her to remember me. Heading to Seattle. You've got my number."

Jokob laid his phone on the table, looked around the RV, and began pulling photos off the shelves, packing them away for travel. He had this routine down and could do it in his sleep. He flipped on his pragmatic side, the same side he'd used to survive the past three years. By five o'clock, he'd secured all the loose items. He pulled deli meat from the fridge and made a sandwich, eating only because he must. He force-swallowed the last bite as the phone rang.

"Kev, thanks for calling back."

"Sure, buddy, what's up?"

Jokob switched to speakerphone and began cleaning up. "Could I come out a little early?"

"Woop! Oh course! That'll give us time to hang before my freedom is forever curtailed by diapers and nighttime feedings."

Jokob chuckled but there was no life in it.

"You okay, bud?"

"Not really, but I will be. I need to get out of here."

"Sure, come on out."

"I may leave tonight. If not, it will be before sun-up tomorrow. Cya in a few days."

thirty

okob!" Julianne spun in a circle, fighting to stay on her feet, screaming into the fierce wind and rain.

"Jewel! Look out!"

In slow motion, Julianne turned to see a wall of murky brown mud-water rushing toward her. She shrieked as it hit her full front and swept her downstream. Covered in mud, she struggled to find air, fearing she would suck in mud if she tried to breathe. The rocks pounded her bones, and tree roots clawed at her as she swirled passed them, ripping her clothes. Her body slammed into the trunk of an uprooted tree.

A scream woke her from a sound sleep. Pitch black, except for some scattered glowing lights. The thuds of her racing heart thumped in her ears. She gasped for air and clawed at her face, like she was trying to wipe something off. *Where am I?* She looked around, willing her eyes to focus, seeking her bearings.

A nurse rushed through the door and flooded the room with intense light. "Are you okay?"

"Where am I?" Julianne rubbed the back of her neck and stared at an unfamiliar woman in light blue scrubs.

"You're at Missouri Baptist Hospital." The nurse placed her fingers on Julianne's wrist and took her pulse. "You've been here for three days and were at Sullivan Regional for nine days before that. You were in an accident.

Don't you remember?"

"Where's Jokob?" Julianne's gaze traced the room, a wave of panic threatening to overwhelm her.

"I'm not sure who that is. This is my first shift since you got here."

"Can you find my mother?"

Her momma slipped through the door to find Julianne sitting on the bed sobbing hysterically. She rushed to her and cradled her in her arms.

"What is it? The nurse said you woke up screaming." Her momma brushed the curls out of Julianne's face.

"He's dead momma. Dead."

"Oh, sweetie, I know it's hard for you to have to go through your poppy's death twice." Her momma pulled back and looked at Julianne.

"Poppy? No, Momma, Jokob. I saw him right before the water hit me." Her breath came in ragged gasps, snot running from her nose, down her chin. "It must've gotten him too."

Her momma held her daughter at arm's length. "Jokob's not dead."

Julianne's eyes jerked wide and she sniffed. "What? Where is he? For that matter, what happened? The last thing I remember was trying to breathe in that muddy water and getting dragged over rocks and branches. Have I been in a coma?"

"Wait, you remember the accident?" Her momma pulled her eyebrows together, jutting her head forward. "You were in and out of consciousness for days. When you came to, you didn't remember the accident or anything from the past six weeks."

Julianne pursed her lips and furrowed her brow. She looked down at her arms, still black and blue, with scabs on long scratch marks. "Am I okay?"

"You suffered a concussion, broken ribs, cuts, and bruises. But, yes, you're okay. The doctor said all the swelling is gone and you're memory would return in its own time. I guess he was right. They're releasing you later today."

"So where is Jokob? The nurse doesn't know him."

"Sweetie." Her momma placed a hand on Julianne's. "You sent him away the day you got here, three days ago."

"What? Why would I do that?" Julianne's voice held a level of panic.

Her momma pulled back the window blinds. The sunlight streamed in, filling the room. She spoke while staring out the window. "I think you broke his heart. He had planned to stay with me, but he got his things and left, with no explanation." She turned back to Julianne. "He sent me a text, saying he was heading to Seattle but hasn't called."

"What? I have to call him." She began looking through the items on her tray table. "Where's my phone?"

"Honey, your phone is probably in the Gulf by now," her momma said, laughing. "Here, use mine."

Jokob steered his RV onto the empty lot next to Kevin's garage.

Kevin was out of the house to greet him before Jokob's feet hit the dirt. "Hey buddy, you made it." He

Jeanne Felfe

wrapped his friend in a bear hug, squeezed and lifted him off the ground. Setting him down, he slapped him on the back.

Jokob stepped back and whistled. "Dude! You've shrunk. You look awesome."

Kevin did a pirouette and held his arms up, like a ballerina. "Only forty more pounds to go. I've never felt this good in my entire life." He laughed and grabbed Jokob's arm. "Come on in, Ammuri can't wait to meet you. She couldn't come outside, Doc says bed rest with her feet up until the baby gets here."

"Everything okay?" Jokob asked, following Kevin into the house, Cooper close behind.

"A little preeclampsia and high blood pressure. She's been trying to control her weight, but the pressure is still too high for safety. But it's all good, the baby is due soon. If needed, they can always take him early."

Jokob had seen photos of Ammuri but nothing prepared him for the exotic beauty, with deep-set obsidian eyes, he encountered lounging on the couch. Her family had migrated from Palestine when she was still in her mother's womb. Her name meant 'captivating,' and he could see why her parents had chosen it.

"Jokob," she called out. "I am so happy to finally meet you. Sorry, I cannot get up, strict rest. It sucks." The light from her smile made him happier than he'd been in days.

He bent to hug her. "Ammuri, you're keeping this big oaf in line, I see. I'm so sorry I missed your wedding."

"Nonsense, you are here now. That is what matters."

Kevin spread his arms and gestured at the room.

242

"Well, this is home, small but ours. Three bedrooms, one for the baby, and one for gaming. Two baths, eat-in kitchen, deck, and fenced yard. Who could ask for more?" He tugged on his chest-length beard and laughed.

Ammuri took Jokob's hand. "You are welcome to park your RV here for your whole stay if you would like. We would love to spend some time with you."

"I might do that."

Kevin disappeared into the kitchen and came back with two beers. "Wanna beer?"

Jokob laughed and reached out. "Must've read my mind." He looked around the room. The swords on the wall intrigued him, and he stepped in for a closer look. "*Lord of the Rings*?"

"Ah, but which character?" Ammuri challenged.

He shrugged his shoulders. "Uh, you got me there."

"Ha, I win." She giggled and clapped her hands like a little girl. "That one is *Andúril*—it is an exact replica of the sword re-forged from the broken pieces of Isildur's sword, *Narsil*. And in that case," she pointed to a glass cabinet behind Jokob, "are *Glamdring*—the sword of Gandalf, a Legolas bow, and *Hadhafang*—Arwen's sword."

He examined each item more closely. "I had forgotten how into *Lord of the Rings* you guys are. This is amazing."

"Oh, there are more in the basement. Kevin's got a full Gandalf costume and I have Galadriel that I hope to be able to fit into by next Halloween, obviously not this one," she said, patting her rounded belly. "And of course we have a tiny Frodo costume for Zander. He will be so cute all wrapped up with huge, furry feet sticking out."

Ammuri shifted on the couch and grabbed her stomach. "Jokob, come quickly. Zander is kicking."

Jokob felt strange touching the belly of woman he'd just met, but did as requested. He bent over and Ammuri pulled his hand onto her stomach. The feeling of the kick startled him and he jerked away. Martin had never kicked. "Oh wow. Doesn't that hurt?"

"Not at all." She pulled her shirt tight across her belly. "Watch this."

The impression of a tiny foot appeared, followed by a wave convulsing across her belly. "Okay, that's a little creepy."

"Just wait, one of these days… " She stopped abruptly and sucked in her breath.

Jokob caught Kevin giving her a slight frown and head-shake.

"Oh I am so sorry, I forgot. I didn't mean—"

He stopped her. "It's okay, I'm happy for you."

Jokob snuggled into the lounger with his second beer when his phone rang. Sibeal's ring. Fearing the worst, he answered on the second ring. "Is Jewel OK?"

"Jokob, it's me, Jewel. Where are you?" Her voice sounded nasally, like she'd been crying.

He shook his head. "Julianne? I don't understand. You told me to leave."

"I know, Momma told me. I woke up from a nightmare and you were gone. I thought you died in the flood. Where are you?"

"I'm in Seattle already."

Julianne drew an audible gasp. "Oh no, I'm so sorry. Momma told me I sent you away because I couldn't remember you. But I remember everything now."

"Wait, you remember everything? You remember… us?" Jokob spoke with hesitation.

"Yes, please, come back."

"I'll be on the next flight out."

thirty-one

Mornin', sleepy head." Jokob tickled Julianne as she tried to duck back under the covers.

"Ugh. It's too early to get up," Julianne said. The previous night's lovemaking had lasted into early dawn. "Ouch."

"I'm sorry. I forgot about your ribs."

"It's okay." She caught him off guard and tickled him back.

Tickling led to kissing and more sweet lovemaking.

Afterward, snuggling contentedly in each other's arms, Jokob said, "Julianne, when you told me to leave the hospital, a part of me died. I didn't know if you would ever remember me again. When you called…" Jokob paused, shaking his head. "I don't ever want to lose you again."

"I'm so sorry, I have no memory of doing that. One minute I was searching for you in the storm, and the next, I woke up in the hospital."

Warm and safe in a way she didn't think she could ever feel again, Julianne rose onto her elbow and kissed him, tracing a hand over his bare chest.

Long silent passions arose again into magical lovemaking.

Jokob hesitated, as they watched the sunset at the bridge where they'd had their first non-date.

"I have to be back in Seattle in a little over a week for my next opening. And I want to be there for Zander's birth, which could be any day now. I missed their wedding, I can't miss this."

Julianne hadn't forgotten about his friend, Kevin. They seemed such an odd match for friends, but they'd met in college and had been tight all these years since.

"I've been trying not to think about it," she replied, her head hung, shoulders slumped. Her emotions threatened to spill from her eyes, as she barely managed to whisper, "I wish you could stay here."

"Come with me," he said, facing her. "You said you've never been to the Pacific Northwest. There are some beautiful places to shoot stories. The idea of leaving you here is tearing me apart. Now that I have you back, I can't imagine going without you.

"Jokob, I can't just pack up my life and leave town. I have a job, I have an apartment, I have *cats*. They wouldn't do so well in an RV, or with Cooper for that matter."

"Jewel, this is my life. It's what I do."

"Well, this is mine," Julianne responded, defiantly.

"Are you sure it's yours? Doesn't sound to me like the one you planned before Clay came along."

Julianne drew back, like she'd been slapped. "That's not fair."

"I shouldn't have said that, but seriously, what does it take beyond a near death experience to wake you up to your heart's desires?"

Julianne silently pondered his words. She stared at the river, no longer swollen from the flooding three weeks ago. Tree trunks, some as large as small cars, drifted past, branches reaching up into the sky. What lay beneath the surface was deadly.

"You may have a point. I need to think about all of this."

The Cup-A-Joe coffee shop across from the hospital was hopping with customers when Julianne arrived. She waited in line to order her double latte with caramel, topped with whipped cream, and kept a lookout for a table. One emptied as she got her order, and she raced to grab it. She mulled over what Jokob had said. It had hurt her feelings, but he was right, she wasn't living the life she'd once dreamed about. She loved nursing, but the days blended into one another. She certainly didn't want to keep doing this all her life, like some of the floor nurses she worked with. There were two that had been there thirty years already, and nursing was hard on the body. Distracted with her thoughts, she didn't notice Bella walk up with her coffee.

"So tell me. What's this big thing you couldn't wait to tell me?"

Julianne chewed her thumbnail. "Jokob leaves within the week and he asked me to go with him." She looked up at Bella, raised her eyebrows, and shrugged.

Bella started running her legs under the table. "OMG! That's so exciting. You're going right? Please tell me you're going."

Julianne tilted her head, rolling her head and her eyes. "I can't just up and run off with a man I've known less than three months."

They stopped talking when the waitress came by to see if they needed anything.

"We're good, thanks," they chimed in unison.

"And why not? You knew Clay for three years before you married him and look what good that did you. Girlfriend, you've gotta follow your heart. Besides, you always said you wanted to travel and do adventurous things. Well, here's your chance."

Julianne stirred her coffee. The swirl of whipped cream made little ripples and disappeared. She looked up and scrunched her mouth to one side. "But, Bella, I've got cats."

"Oh my gawd! You're gonna let cats stand in the way of true love? Are you nuts? Geez, *I'll* keep them for you until you get back."

"Yeah right, you don't even like cats."

"For you, I'll make an exception. Besides, I love Ben and Jerry's." Bella's laughter jiggled her newly showing baby bump.

Julianne laughed, too, knowing Bella's one true weakness, besides Alessandro, was good, rich ice cream.

"Bella, this isn't a carton of *Chunky Monkey*, these are real live cats that climb on furniture and counters and have a litter box and—"

Bella held up her hand and interrupted her friend. "I said I'd keep them. Nicky and Isabella will love having kitties to play with."

Bella munched on her biscotti. "Besides, you could always fly out to Seattle, stay a couple of weeks, and come home. Doesn't have to be an all or nothing decision. You always do that, never any gray area with you."

"I suppose you're right, but I don't know if I can take off given I was out on disability for three weeks. I've only been back at work a week."

"You never know if you don't ask."

After they parted ways outside the coffee shop, Julianne strolled the few blocks to the St. Louis Zoo, one of her favorite places to think. She usually gravitated to the tigers. Not sure why, but something about them always brought her peace and clarity. She wrapped her hands around the outer bar of the enclosure and talked to Bing, the female.

"So, Bing, what do you think I should do?"

Bing stared back with her jungle cat eyes, panting and grunting her jungle cat gruff.

Julianne walked over to the bench across from the enclosure. Bing lay on the rocks, three cubs climbing over her. She loved her job but had felt for a long time that something was missing. She thought about what Jokob had said… *is he right? Am I living my own life? Well, certainly not the one I planned. I want to work but don't absolutely have to for a while, due to my inheritance from Nonna. Putting that money away gave me options. But what would Nonna think of me using it to travel?*

"What do you think, Bing?"

Bing grunted back.

I love Jokob, and the idea of traveling with him is appealing. But what would I do all day while he's out shooting? Going on location with him was fun, but that's his life, not mine. Is he trying to recreate the life he had with Keara? That thought had been darkening her mood. *What if I can't be what he needs? I'm not Keara.*

As she watched the tiger cubs play, a peace came over her.

"I know exactly what to do. Thanks, Bing."

Julianne sprinted to her car and drove the two blocks to the hospital parking garage. Chewing her thumbnail, she waited for the elevator, tapping the button multiple times. *Hurry up.* One, two… eight more to go. *I can't wait.* She raced for the stairs, taking them at a full gallop.

Reaching the third floor, she waited with her hand on the knob, sucking in oxygen, trying to calm herself. *What if they say no? I hadn't thought about that. That can't happen. I have to be firm.*

She ran her fingers through her curls, pulled her shoulders back and opened the stairwell door. She strolled to HR, deliberately slowing her steps. She paused at the door. *What if I'm wrong about this? I was wrong about Clay, wrong to set my own dreams aside for his.*

Shaking her negativity aside, Julianne twisted the knob and stepped in…

Five weeks after nearly dying in the flood, Julianne dragged two suitcases out of Bella's trunk.

"Bella, are you sure about the cats?" Julianne asked, as the skycap loaded the last of her luggage onto the cart. Bella's car idled in a five-minute passenger drop-off slot by the United Airline curb check-in.

"Go! The cats will be fine." Bella hugged her friend.

"But I don't know when I'll be back."

"Well, if you never return, then I guess I've got cats." Bella laughed, as she tipped the skycap.

A security guard gestured in their direction.

"I've got to roll before they run me off. Get outta

here before you miss your flight." She gave Julianne a last quick hug.

Julianne took her rolling bag and headed toward the automatic doors. She glanced over her shoulder and waved goodbye.

In the main terminal, she studied the flight board. She finally found United flight 3521 to Denver. On-time. Gate 31 C.

She paused before entering the security check-in line. "Jewel."

She looked over the heads of the other travelers to see the ruggedly handsome face she'd come to love hurrying toward her.

"Glad I caught you," he said, hands on his knees, breathless and panting from running.

"Jokob, what are you doing here?" she said in total surprise. They had said their goodbyes the day before with sweet and passionate lovemaking. She hadn't expected to see him at the airport at five in the morning. "Your flight isn't until this afternoon."

"I had to give you something before you left," he said, taking her in his arms and kissing her, long, slow, and deep.

"That, and this." Jokob looked around for a secluded spot and guided her by her elbow. "Close your eyes and hold out your hand."

Julianne raised her eyebrows and grinned, but did as he asked. He placed something cool and smooth in her palm.

"Now, open."

She opened her eyes to find a crystal-green, heart shaped stone in her palm. It was about the size of a nickel around. She picked it up with her other hand and held it up to the light. It glistened when she rotated it. She looked at Jokob and he was holding an equally brilliant blue stone up to the light.

"These are heart stones. Carry it with you to help keep me close, I will carry yours." He laid his stone in his palm, placed his flat hand over Julianne's heart, and guided her to place her palm with the stone over his heart.

"Breathe into the stone and imagine filling it with your love," he directed.

They both closed their eyes and drifted into their hearts. Each took a deep breath and reopened their glistening eyes.

"I don't know about you," Jokob said, "but that was one of the most amazing experiences I've ever had. I felt like I was being drawn into your heart and surrounded by love."

Julianne pulled in a deep, slow breath, still in that magical place. She wasn't quite sure what had happened, but joy filled her from head to toe. She put her arms around him and placed her head on his chest, listening to the beating of his heart, trying to memorize the cadence.

Jokob pulled back. "You'd better go. Don't want you to miss your flight. But first, I have something else for you," he said, handing her the camera he'd loaned her on their first non-date. "Shoot lots of stories."

"And one last thing." He laughed and handed her a huge bag of candy. "The kids are gonna love you. I know I do." He cupped her cheek in his palm and grinned at her.

"Your love is what gives me the courage to follow my dream. I love you too. I'm going to miss you so much." Tears threatened to spill again, as she grazed his cheek with the back of her hand and gazed into his eyes, seeking to commit each feature to memory. She grabbed her rolling bag and headed for the security checkpoint.

"We'll Skype if you have access. Call me when you get there. I love you," he called after her.

Nearing the corner toward her gate, Julianne looked over her shoulder and flashed Jokob a brilliant smile. She disappeared, feeling the excited rush of the future, as she finally picked up the shattered pieces of her old dreams, those of the life she'd wanted to live, and headed toward the possibility of new ones. When she reached the seating area for her flight, she pulled a manila envelope out of her carry-on bag. The label on the outside read *Sisters of Mercy, Roatan, Honduras.*

Jokob watched Julianne until she completed the security check and disappeared around the corner, staying long enough to catch one last smile. He strolled contentedly out to his rental car. He planned to drive around Old Town St. Charles while waiting for his flight to Seattle to meet his Godson, Zander. He'd delayed his opening for a week to take care of some unfinished business.

One week later, Jokob guided his rental onto the grounds of Holy Sacred Memories. Checking the map to locate the site, he wound through the trees and headstones.

255

He found section S332 and pulled the car to the side of the narrow road. Stepping out of the vehicle, he reached back inside and removed what he'd brought. He wandered past headstones scarred by time. He came to one newer, but with the grass fully grown. Sitting in front of the ornate granite stone, he placed a single white rose in the vase. He fingered the writing on the stone—*Keara Morgan O'Callaghan* and *Martin O'Callaghan*.

"Keara," Jokob spoke hesitantly. "I'm sorry I haven't been here. It was all too much. I'm better now. I found the bridge, Keara. I found Jewel, like your poem said I would. I think you would like her."

The End

Made in the USA
Lexington, KY
29 April 2017